Yvette

by

Henri Rene Guy De Maupassant

Yvette
by Henri Rene Guy De Maupassant

ISBN: 978-93-69070-73-2

Published by

DOUBLE 9 BOOKS

2/13-B, Ansari Road
Daryaganj, New Delhi – 110002
info@double9books.com
www.double9books.com
Tel. 011-40042856

ABOUT THE AUTHOR

Henri René Albert Guy de Maupassant was a prominent French author born on August 5, 1850, at Château de Miromesnil in Tourville-sur-Arques, France. Renowned for his mastery of the short story, Maupassant was a leading figure in the naturalist movement, which sought to depict human lives and social conditions in stark, often pessimistic terms. His works frequently explored the darker aspects of life, revealing the complex interplay of human nature, fate, and social forces. Maupassant was greatly influenced by his literary mentors, including Gustave Flaubert, Émile Zola, and Honoré de Balzac, as well as the philosophical ideas of Arthur Schopenhauer. After studying at the Lycée Pierre-Corneille and Lycée Henri-IV, he went on to attend the University of Paris. Maupassant's prolific writing career produced numerous short stories, novels, and essays, many of which reflect his disillusionment with society and the human condition. Some of his most famous works include Boule de Suif and The Necklace. Maupassant's life, however, was marked by personal struggles, and he died prematurely on July 6, 1893, at the age of 42, in Passy, Paris, likely due to complications from syphilis. His legacy as a master of literary realism endures today.

ABOUT THE AUTHOR

Henri René Albert Guy de Maupassant was a prominent French author born on August 5, 1850, at Château de Miromesnil in Tourville-sur-Arques, France. Renowned for his mastery of the short story, Maupassant was a leading figure in the naturalist movement, which sought to depict human lives and social conditions in stark, often pessimistic terms. His works frequently explored the darker aspects of life, revealing the complex interplay of human nature, fate, and social forces. Maupassant was greatly influenced by his literary mentors, including Gustave Flaubert, Émile Zola, and Honoré de Balzac, as well as the philosophical ideas of Arthur Schopenhauer. After studying at the Lycée Pierre-Corneille and Lycée Henri-IV, he went on to attend the University of Paris. Maupassant's prolific writing career produced numerous short stories, novels, and essays, many of which reflect his disillusionment with society and the human condition. Some of his most famous works include Boule de Suif and The Necklace. Maupassant's life, however, was marked by personal struggles, and he died prematurely on July 6, 1893, at the age of 42, in Passy, Paris, likely due to complications from syphilis. His legacy as a master of literary realism endures today.

CONTENTS

CHAPTER I
THE INITIATION OF SAVAL

As they were leaving the Cafe Riche, Jean de Servigny said to Leon Saval: "If you don't object, let us walk. The weather is too fine to take a cab."

His friend answered: "I would like nothing better."

Jean replied: "It is hardly eleven o'clock. We shall arrive much before midnight, so let us go slowly."

A restless crowd was moving along the boulevard, that throng peculiar to summer nights, drinking, chatting, and flowing like a river, filled with a sense of comfort and joy. Here and there a cafe threw a flood of light upon a knot of patrons drinking at little tables on the sidewalk, which were covered with bottles and glasses, hindering the passing of the hurrying multitude. On the pavement the cabs with their red, blue, or green lights dashed by, showing for a second, in the glimmer, the thin shadow of the horse, the raised profile of the coachman, and the dark box of the carriage. The cabs of the Urbaine Company made clear and rapid spots when their yellow panels were struck by the light.

The two friends walked with slow steps, cigars in their mouths, in evening dress and overcoats on their arms, with a flower in their buttonholes, and their hats a trifle on one side, as men will carelessly wear them sometimes, after they have dined well and the air is mild.

They had been linked together since their college days by a close, devoted, and firm affection. Jean de Servigny, small, slender, a trifle bald, rather frail, with elegance of mien, curled mustache, bright eyes, and fine lips, was a man who seemed born and bred upon the boulevard. He was tireless in spite of his languid air, strong in spite of his pallor, one of those slight Parisians to whom gymnastic exercise, fencing, cold shower and hot baths give a nervous, artificial strength. He was known by his marriage as well as by his wit, his fortune, his connections, and by that sociability, amiability, and fashionable gallantry peculiar to certain men.

A true Parisian, furthermore, light, sceptical, changeable, captivating, energetic, and irresolute, capable of everything and of nothing; selfish by principle and generous on occasion, he lived moderately upon his income, and amused himself with hygiene. Indifferent and passionate, he gave himself rein and drew back constantly, impelled by conflicting instincts, yielding to all, and then obeying, in the end, his own shrewd man-about-town judgment, whose weather-vane logic consisted in following the wind and drawing profit from circumstances without taking the trouble to originate them.

His companion, Leon Saval, rich also, was one of those superb and colossal figures who make women turn around in the streets to look at them. He gave the idea of a statue turned into a man, a type of a race, like those sculptured forms which are sent to the Salons. Too handsome, too tall, too big, too strong, he sinned a little from the excess of everything, the excess of his qualities. He had on hand countless affairs of passion.

As they reached the Vaudeville theater, he asked: "Have you warned that lady that you are going to take me to her house to see her?"

Servigny began to laugh: "Forewarn the Marquise Obardi! Do you warn an omnibus driver that you shall enter his stage at the corner of the boulevard?"

Saval, a little perplexed, inquired: "What sort of person is this lady?"

His friend replied: "An upstart, a charming hussy, who came from no one knows where, who made her appearance one day, nobody knows how, among the adventuresses of Paris, knowing perfectly well how to take care of herself. Besides, what difference does it make to us? They say that her real name, her maiden name—for she still has every claim to the title of maiden except that of innocence—is Octavia Bardin, from which she constructs the name Obardi by prefixing the first letter of her first name and dropping the last letter of the last name."

"Moreover, she is a lovable woman, and you, from your physique, are inevitably bound to become her lover. Hercules is not introduced into Messalina's home without making some disturbance. Nevertheless I make bold to add that if there is free entrance to this house, just as there is in bazaars, you are not exactly compelled to buy what is for sale. Love and cards are on the programme, but nobody compels you to take up with either. And the exit is as free as the entrance."

"She settled down in the Etoile district, a suspicious neighborhood, three years ago, and opened her drawing-room to that froth of the continents which comes to Paris to practice its various formidable and criminal talents."

"I don't remember just how I went to her house. I went as we all go, because there is card playing, because the women are compliant, and the men dishonest. I love that social mob of buccaneers with decorations of all sorts of orders, all titled, and all entirely unknown at their embassies, except to the spies. They are always dragging in the subject of honor, quoting the list of their ancestors on the slightest provocation, and telling the story of their life at every opportunity, braggarts, liars, sharpers, dangerous as their cards, false as their names, brave because they have to be, like the assassins who can not pluck their victims except by exposing their own lives. In a word, it is the aristocracy of the bagnio."

"I like them. They are interesting to fathom and to know, amusing to listen to, often witty, never commonplace as the ordinary French guests. Their women are always pretty, with a little flavor of foreign knavery, with the mystery of their past existence, half of which, perhaps, spent in a House of Correction. They generally have fine eyes and glorious hair, the true physique of the profession, an intoxicating grace, a seductiveness which drives men to folly, an unwholesome, irresistible charm! They conquer like the highwaymen of old. They are rapacious creatures; true birds of prey. I like them, too."

"The Marquise Obardi is one of the type of these elegant good-for-nothings. Ripe and pretty, with a feline charm, you can see that she is vicious to the marrow. Everybody has a good time at her house, with cards, dancing, and suppers; in fact there is everything which goes to make up the pleasures of fashionable society life."

"Have you ever been or are you now her lover?" Leon Saval asked.

"I have not been her lover, I am not now, and I never shall be. I only go to the house to see her daughter."

"Ah! She has a daughter, then?"

"A daughter! A marvel, my dear man. She is the principal attraction of the den to-day. Tall, magnificent, just ripe, eighteen years old, as fair as her mother is dark, always merry, always ready for an entertainment, always laughing, and ready to dance like mad. Who will be the lucky man, to capture her, or who has already done so? Nobody can tell that. She has ten of us in her train, all hoping."

"Such a daughter in the hands of a woman like the Marquise is a fortune. And they play the game together, the two charmers. No one knows just what they are planning. Perhaps they are waiting for a better bargain than I should prove. But I tell you that I shall close the bargain if I ever get a chance."

"That girl Yvette absolutely baffles me, moreover. She is a mystery. If she is not the most complete monster of astuteness and perversity that I have ever seen, she certainly is the most marvelous phenomenon of innocence that can be imagined. She lives in that atmosphere of infamy with a calm and triumphing ease which is either wonderfully profligate or entirely artless. Strange scion of an adventuress, cast upon the muck-heap of that set, like a magnificent plant nurtured upon corruption, or rather like the daughter of some noble race, of some great artist, or of some grand lord, of some prince or dethroned king, tossed some evening into her mother's arms, nobody can make out what she is nor what she thinks. But you are going to see her."

Saval began to laugh and said: "You are in love with her."

"No. I am on the list, which is not precisely the same thing. I will introduce you to my most serious rivals. But the chances are in my favor. I am in the lead, and some little distinction is shown to me."

"You are in love," Saval repeated.

"No. She disquiets me, seduces and disturbs me, attracts and frightens me away. I mistrust her as I would a trap, and I long for her as I long for a sherbet when I am thirsty. I yield to her charm, and I only approach her with the apprehension that I would feel concerning a man who was known to be a skillful thief. To her presence I have an irrational impulse toward belief in her possible purity and a very reasonable mistrust of her not less probable trickery. I feel myself in contact with an abnormal being, beyond the pale of natural laws, an exquisite or detestable creature—I don't know which."

For the third time Saval said: "I tell you that you are in love. You speak of her with the magniloquence of a poet and the feeling of a troubadour. Come, search your heart, and confess."

Servigny walked a few steps without answering. Then he replied:

"That is possible, after all. In any case, she fills my mind almost continually. Yes, perhaps I am in love. I dream about her too much. I think of her when I am asleep and when I awake—that is surely a grave indication. Her face follows me, accompanies me ceaselessly, ever before me, around me, with me. Is this love, this physical infatuation? Her features are so stamped upon my vision that I see her the moment I shut my eyes. My heart beats quickly every time I look at her, I don't deny it."

"So I am in love with her, but in a queer fashion. I have the strongest desire for her, and yet the idea of making her my wife would seem to me a folly, a piece of stupidity, a monstrous thing: And I have a little fear of her, as well, the fear which a bird feels over which a hawk is hovering."

"And again I am jealous of her, jealous of all of which I am ignorant in her incomprehensible heart. I am always wondering: 'Is she a charming youngster or a wretched jade?' She says things that would make an army shudder; but so does a parrot. She is at times so indiscreet and yet modest that I am forced to believe in her spotless purity, and again so incredibly artless that I must suspect that she has never been chaste. She allures me, excites me, like a woman of a certain category, and at the same time acts like an impeccable virgin. She seems to love me and yet makes fun of me; she deports herself in public as if she were my mistress and treats me in private as if I were her brother or footman."

"There are times when I fancy that she has as many lovers as her mother. And at other times I imagine that she suspects absolutely nothing of that sort of life, you understand. Furthermore, she is a great novel reader. I am at present, while awaiting something better, her book purveyor. She calls me her 'librarian.' Every week the New Book Store sends her, on my orders, everything new that has appeared, and I believe that she reads everything at random. It must make a strange sort of mixture in her head."

"That kind of literary hasty-pudding accounts perhaps for some of the girl's peculiar ways. When a young woman looks at existence through the medium of fifteen thousand novels, she must see it in a strange light, and construct queer ideas about matters and things in general. As for me, I am waiting. It is certain at any rate that I never have had for any other woman the devotion which I have had for her. And still it is quite certain that I shall never marry her. So if she has had numbers, I shall swell the number. And if she has not, I shall take the first ticket, just as I would do for a street car."

"The case is very simple. Of course, she will never marry. Who in the world would marry the Marquise Obardi's daughter, the child of Octavia Bardin? Nobody, for a thousand reasons. Where would they ever find a husband for her? In society? Never. The mother's house is a sort of liberty-hall whose patronage is attracted by the daughter. Girls don't get married under those conditions."

"Would she find a husband among the trades-people? Still less would that be possible. And besides the Marquise is not the woman to make a bad bargain; she will give Yvette only to a man of high position, and that man she will never discover."

"Then perhaps she will look among the common people. Still less likely. There is no solution of the problem, then. This young lady belongs neither to society, nor to the tradesmen's class, nor to the common people, and she can never enter any of these ranks by marriage."

"She belongs through her mother, her birth, her education, her inheritance, her manners, and her customs, to the vortex of the most rapid life of Paris. She can never escape it, save by becoming a nun, which is not at all probable with her manners and tastes. She has only one possible career, a life of pleasure. She will come to it sooner or later, if indeed she has not already begun to tread its primrose path. She cannot escape her fate. From being a young girl she will take the inevitable step, quite simply. And I would like to be the pivot of this transformation."

"I am waiting. There are many lovers. You will see among them a Frenchman, Monsieur de Belvigne; a Russian, called Prince Kravalow, and an Italian, Chevalier Valreali, who have all announced their candidacies and who are consequently maneuvering to the best of their ability. In addition to these there are several freebooters of less importance. The Marquise waits and watches. But I think that she has views about me. She knows that I am very rich, and she makes less of the others."

"Her drawing-room is, moreover, the most astounding that I know of, in such, exhibitions. You even meet very decent men there, like ourselves. As for the women, she has culled the best there is from the basket of pickpockets. Nobody knows where she found them. It is a set apart from Bohemia, apart from everything. She has had one inspiration showing genius, and that is the knack of selecting especially those adventuresses who have children, generally girls. So that a fool might believe that in her house he was among respectable women!" They had reached the avenue of the Champs-Elysees. A gentle breeze softly stirred the leaves and touched the faces of passers-by, like the breaths of a giant fan, waving somewhere in the sky. Silent shadows wandered beneath the trees; others, on benches, made a dark spot. And these shadows spoke very low, as if they were telling each other important or shameful secrets.

"You can't imagine what a collection of fictitious titles are met in this lair," said Servigny, "By the way, I shall present you by the name of Count Saval; plain Saval would not do at all."

"Oh, no, indeed!" cried his friend; "I would not have anyone think me capable of borrowing a title, even for an evening, even among those people. Ah, no!"

Servigny began to laugh.

"How stupid you are! Why, in that set they call me the Duke de Servigny. I don't know how nor why. But at any rate the Duke de Servigny I am and shall remain, without complaining or protesting. It does not worry me. I should have no footing there whatever without a title."

But Saval would not be convinced.

"Well, you are of rank, and so you may remain. But, as for me, no. I shall be the only common person in the drawing-room. So much the worse, or, so much the better. It will be my mark of distinction and superiority."

Servigny was obstinate.

"I tell you that it is not possible. Why, it would almost seem monstrous. You would have the effect of a ragman at a meeting of emperors. Let me do as I like. I shall introduce you as the Vice-Roi du 'Haut-Mississippi,' and no one will be at all astonished. When a man takes on greatness, he can't take too much."

"Once more, no, I do not wish it."

"Very well, have your way. But, in fact, I am very foolish to try to convince you. I defy you to get in without some one giving you a title, just as they give a bunch of violets to the ladies at the entrance to certain stores."

They turned to the right in the Rue de Barrie, mounted one flight of stairs in a fine modern house, and gave their overcoats and canes into the hands of four servants in knee-breeches. A warm odor, as of a festival assembly, filled the air, an odor of flowers, perfumes, and women; and a composed and continuous murmur came from the adjoining rooms, which were filled with people.

A kind of master of ceremonies, tall, erect, wide of girth, serious, his face framed in white whiskers, approached the newcomers, asking with a short and haughty bow: "Whom shall I announce?"

"Monsieur Saval," Servigny replied.

Then with a loud voice, the man opening the door cried out to the crowd of guests:

"Monsieur the Duke de Servigny."

"Monsieur the Baron Saval."

The first drawing-room was filled with women. The first thing which attracted attention was the display of bare shoulders, above a flood of brilliant gowns.

The mistress of the house who stood talking with three friends, turned and came forward with a majestic step, with grace in her mien and a smile on her lips. Her forehead was narrow and very low, and was covered with a mass of glossy black hair, encroaching a little upon the temples.

She was tall, a trifle too large, a little too stout, over ripe, but very pretty, with a heavy, warm, potent beauty. Beneath that mass of hair, full of dreams and smiles, rendering her mysteriously captivating, were enormous black eyes. Her nose was a little narrow, her mouth large and infinitely seductive, made to speak and to conquer.

Her greatest charm was in her voice. It came from that mouth as water from a spring, so natural, so light, so well modulated, so clear, that there was a physical pleasure in listening to it. It was a joy for the ear to hear the flexible words flow with the grace of a babbling brook, and it was a joy for the eyes to see those pretty lips, a trifle too red, open as the words rippled forth.

She gave one hand to Servigny, who kissed it, and dropping her fan on its little gold chain, she gave the other to Saval, saying to him: "You are welcome, Baron, all the Duke's friends are at home here."

Then she fixed her brilliant eyes upon the Colossus who had just been introduced to her. She had just the slightest down on her upper lip, a suspicion of a mustache, which seemed darker when she spoke. There was a pleasant odor about her, pervading, intoxicating, some perfume of America or of the Indies. Other people came in, marquesses, counts or princes. She said to Servigny, with the graciousness of a mother: "You will find my daughter in the other parlor. Have a good time, gentlemen, the house is yours."

And she left them to go to those who had come later, throwing at Saval that smiling and fleeting glance which women use to show that they are pleased. Servigny grasped his friend's arm.

"I will pilot you," said he. "In this parlor where we now are, women, the temples of the fleshly, fresh or otherwise. Bargains as good as new, even better, for sale or on lease. At the right, gaming, the temple of money. You understand all about that. At the lower end, dancing, the temple of innocence, the sanctuary, the market for young girls. They are shown off there in every light. Even legitimate marriages are tolerated. It is the future, the hope, of our evenings. And the most curious part of this museum of moral diseases are these young girls whose souls are out of joint, just like the limbs of the little clowns born of mountebanks. Come and look at them."

He bowed, right and left, courteously, a compliment on his lips, sweeping each low-gowned woman whom he knew with the look of an expert.

The musicians, at the end of the second parlor, were playing a waltz; and the two friends stopped at the door to look at them. A score of couples were whirling-the men with a serious expression, and the women with a fixed smile on their lips. They displayed a good deal of shoulder, like their mothers; and the bodices of some were only held in place by a slender ribbon, disclosing at times more than is generally shown.

Suddenly from the end of the room a tall girl darted forward, gliding through the crowd, brushing against the dancers, and holding her long train in her left hand. She ran with quick little steps as women do in crowds, and called out: "Ah! How is Muscade? How do you do, Muscade?"

Her features wore an expression of the bloom of life, the illumination of happiness. Her white flesh seemed to shine, the golden-white flesh which goes with red hair. The mass of her tresses, twisted on her head, fiery, flaming locks, nestled against her supple neck, which was still a little thin.

She seemed to move just as her mother was made to speak, so natural, noble, and simple were her gestures. A person felt a moral joy and physical pleasure in seeing her walk, stir about, bend her head, or lift her arm. "Ah! Muscade, how do you do, Muscade?" she repeated.

Servigny shook her hand violently, as he would a man's, and said: "Mademoiselle Yvette, my friend, Baron Saval."

"Good evening, Monsieur. Are you always as tall as that?"

Servigny replied in that bantering tone which he always used with her, in order to conceal his mistrust and his uncertainty:

"No, Mam'zelle. He has put on his greatest dimensions to please your mother, who loves a colossus."

And the young girl remarked with a comic seriousness: "Very well But when you come to see me you must diminish a little if you please. I prefer the medium height. Now Muscade has just the proportions which I like."

And she gave her hand to the newcomer. Then she asked: "Do you dance, Muscade? Come, let us waltz." Without replying, with a quick movement, passionately, Servigny clasped her waist and they disappeared with the fury of a whirlwind.

They danced more rapidly than any of the others, whirled and whirled, and turned madly, so close together that they seemed but one, and with the form erect, the legs almost motionless, as if some invisible mechanism, concealed beneath their feet, caused them to twirl. They appeared tireless. The other dancers stopped from time to time. They still danced on, alone. They seemed not to know where they were nor what they were doing, as if, they had gone far away from the ball, in an ecstasy. The musicians continued to play, with their looks fixed upon this mad couple; all the guests gazed at them, and when finally they did stop dancing, everyone applauded them.

She was a little flushed, with strange eyes, ardent and timid, less daring than a moment before, troubled eyes, blue, yet with a pupil so black that they seemed hardly natural. Servigny appeared giddy. He leaned against a door to regain his composure.

"You have no head, my poor Muscade, I am steadier than you," said Yvette to Servigny. He smiled nervously, and devoured her with a look. His animal feelings revealed themselves in his eyes and in the curl of his lips. She stood beside him looking down, and her bosom rose and fell in short gasps as he looked at her.

Then she said softly: "Really, there are times when you are like a tiger about to spring upon his prey. Come, give me your arm, and let us find your friend."

Silently he offered her his arm and they went down the long drawing-room together.

Saval was not alone, for the Marquise Obardi had rejoined him. She conversed with him on ordinary and fashionable subjects with a seductiveness in her tones which intoxicated him. And, looking at her with his mental eye, it seemed to him that her lips, uttered words far different from those which they formed. When she saw Servigny her face immediately lighted up, and turning toward him she said:

"You know, my dear Duke, that I have just leased a villa at Bougival for two months, and I count upon your coming to see me there, and upon your friend also. Listen. We take possession next Monday, and shall expect both of you to dinner the following Saturday. We shall keep you over Sunday."

Perfectly serene and tranquil Yvette smiled, saying with a decision which swept away hesitation on his part:

"Of course Muscade will come to dinner on Saturday. We have only to ask him, for he and I intend to commit a lot of follies in the country."

He thought he divined the birth of a promise in her smile, and in her voice he heard what he thought was invitation.

Then the Marquise turned her big, black eyes upon Saval: "And you will, of course, come, Baron?"

With a smile that forbade doubt, he bent toward her, saying, "I shall be only too charmed, Madame."

Then Yvette murmured with malice that was either naive or traitorous: "We will set all the world by the ears down there, won't we, Muscade, and make my regiment of admirers fairly mad." And with a look, she pointed out a group of men who were looking at them from a little distance.

Said Servigny to her: "As many follies as YOU may please, Mam'zelle."

In speaking to Yvette, Servigny never used the word "Mademoiselle," by reason of his close and long intimacy with her.

Then Saval asked: "Why does Mademoiselle always call my friend Servigny 'Muscade'?"

Yvette assumed a very frank air and said:

"I will tell you: It is because he always slips through my hands. Now I think I have him, and then I find I have not."

The Marquise, with her eyes upon Saval, arid evidently preoccupied, said in a careless tone: "You children are very funny."

But Yvette bridled up: "I do not intend to be funny; I am simply frank. Muscade pleases me, and is always deserting me, and that is what annoys me."

Servigny bowed profoundly, saying: "I will never leave you any more, Mam'zelle, neither day nor night." She made a gesture of horror:

"My goodness! no—what do you mean? You are all right during the day, but at night you might embarrass me."

With an air of impertinence he asked: "And why?"

Yvette responded calmly and audaciously, "Because you would not look well en deshabille."

The Marquise, without appearing at all disturbed, said: "What extraordinary subjects for conversation. One would think that you were not at all ignorant of such things."

And Servigny jokingly added: "That is also my opinion, Marquise."

Yvette turned her eyes upon him, and in a haughty, yet wounded, tone said: "You are becoming very vulgar—just as you have been several times lately." And turning quickly she appealed to an individual standing by:

"Chevalier, come and defend me from insult."

A thin, brown man, with an easy carriage, came forward.

"Who is the culprit?" said he, with a constrained smile.

Yvette pointed out Servigny with a nod of her head:

"There he is, but I like him better than I do you, because he is less of a bore."

The Chevalier Valreali bowed:

"I do what I can, Mademoiselle. I may have less ability, but not less devotion."

A gentleman came forward, tall and stout, with gray whiskers, saying in loud tones: "Mademoiselle Yvette, I am your most devoted slave."

Yvette cried: "Ah, Monsieur de Belvigne." Then turning toward Saval, she introduced him.

"My last adorer—big, fat, rich, and stupid. Those are the kind I like. A veritable drum-major—but of the table d'hote. But see, you are still bigger than he. How shall I nickname you? Good! I have it. I shall call you 'M. Colossus of Rhodes, Junior,' from the Colossus who certainly was your father. But you two ought to have very interesting things to say to each other up there, above the heads of us all—so, by-bye."

And she left them quickly, going to the orchestra to make the musicians strike up a quadrille.

Madame Obardi seemed preoccupied. In a soft voice she said to Servigny:

"You are always teasing her. You will warp her character and bring out many bad traits."

Servigny replies: "Why, haven't you finished her education?"

She appeared not to understand, and continued talking in a friendly way. But she noticed a solemn looking man, wearing a perfect constellation of crosses and orders, standing near her, and she ran to him:

"Ah Prince, Prince, what good fortune!"

Servigny took Saval's arm and drew him away:

"That is the latest serious suitor, Prince Kravalow. Isn't she superb?"

"To my mind they are both superb. The mother would suffice for me perfectly," answered Saval.

Servigny nodded and said: "At your disposal, my dear boy."

The dancers elbowed them aside, as they were forming for a quadrille.

"Now let us go and see the sharpers," said Servigny. And they entered the gambling-room.

Around each table stood a group of men, looking on. There was very little conversation. At times the clink of gold coins, tossed upon the green cloth or hastily seized, added its sound to the murmur of the players, just as if the money was putting in its word among the human voices.

All the men were decorated with various orders, and odd ribbons, and they all wore the same severe expression, with different countenances. The especially distinguishing feature was the beard.

The stiff American with his horseshoe, the haughty Englishman with his fan-beard open on his breast, the Spaniard with his black fleece reaching to the eyes, the Roman with that huge mustache which Italy copied from Victor Emmanuel, the Austrian with his whiskers and shaved chin, a Russian general whose lip seemed armed with two twisted lances, and a Frenchman with a dainty mustache, displayed the fancies of all the barbers in the world.

"You won't join the game?" asked Servigny.

"No, shall you?"

"Not now. If you are ready to go, we will come back some quieter day. There are too many people here to-day, and we can't do anything."

"Well, let us go."

And they disappeared behind a door-curtain into the hall. As soon as they were in the street Servigny asked: "Well, what do you think of it?"

"It certainly is interesting, but I fancy the women's side of it more than the men's."

"Indeed! Those women are the best of the tribe for us. Don't you find that you breathe the odor of love among them, just as you scent the perfumes at a hairdresser's?"

"Really such houses are the place for one to go. And what experts, my dear fellow! What artists! Have you ever eaten bakers' cakes? They look well, but they amount to nothing. The man who bakes them only knows how to make bread. Well! the love of a woman in ordinary society always reminds me of these bake-shop trifles, while the love you find at houses like the Marquise Obardi's, don't you see, is the real sweetmeat. Oh! they know how to make cakes, these charming pastry-cooks. Only you pay five sous, at their shops, for what costs two sous elsewhere."

"Who is the master of the house just now?" asked Saval.

Servigny shrugged his shoulders, signifying his ignorance.

"I don't know, the latest one known was an English peer, but he left three months ago. At present she must live off the common herd, or the gambling, perhaps, and on the gamblers, for she has her caprices. But tell me, it is understood that we dine with her on Saturday at Bougival, is it not?

People are more free in the country, and I shall succeed in finding out what ideas Yvette has in her head!"

"I should like nothing better," replied Saval. "I have nothing to do that day."

Passing down through the Champs-Elysees, under the steps they disturbed a couple making love on one of the benches, and Servigny muttered: "What foolishness and what a serious matter at the same time! How commonplace and amusing love is, always the same and always different! And the beggar who gives his sweetheart twenty sous gets as much return as I would for ten thousand francs from some Obardi, no younger and no less stupid perhaps than this nondescript. What nonsense!"

He said nothing for a few minutes; then he began again: "All the same, it would be good to become Yvette's first lover. Oh! for that I would give—"

He did not add what he would give, and Saval said good night to him as they reached the corner of the Rue Royale.

CHAPTER II
BOUGIVAL AND LOVE

They had set the table on the veranda which overlooked the river. The Printemps villa, leased by the Marquise Obardi, was halfway up this hill, just at the corner of the Seine, which turned before the garden wall, flowing toward Marly.

Opposite the residence, the island of Croissy formed a horizon of tall trees, a mass of verdure, and they could see a long stretch of the big river as far as the floating cafe of La Grenouillere hidden beneath the foliage.

The evening fell, one of those calm evenings at the waterside, full of color yet soft, one of those peaceful evenings which produces a sensation of pleasure. No breath of air stirred the branches, no shiver of wind ruffled the smooth clear surface of the Seine. It was not too warm, it was mild—good weather to live in. The grateful coolness of the banks of the Seine rose toward a serene sky.

The sun disappeared behind the trees to shine on other lands, and one seemed to absorb the serenity of the already sleeping earth, to inhale, in the peace of space, the life of the infinite.

As they left the drawing-room to seat themselves at the table everyone was joyous. A softened gaiety filled their hearts, they felt that it would be so delightful to dine there in the country, with that great river and that twilight for a setting, breathing that pure and fragrant air.

The Marquise had taken Saval's arm, and Yvette, Servigny's. The four were alone by themselves. The two women seemed entirely different persons from what they were at Paris, especially Yvette. She talked but little, and seemed languid and grave.

Saval, hardly recognizing her in this frame of mind, asked her: "What is the matter, Mademoiselle? I find you changed since last week. You have become quite a serious person."

"It is the country that does that for me," she replied. "I am not the same, I feel queer; besides I am never two days alike. To-day I have the air of a mad woman, and to-morrow shall be as grave as an elegy. I change with the weather, I don't know why. You see, I am capable of anything, according to the moment. There are days when I would like to kill people,—not animals, I would never kill animals,—but people, yes, and other days when I weep at a mere thing. A lot of different ideas pass through my head. It depends, too, a good deal on how I get up. Every morning, on waking, I can tell just what I shall be in the evening. Perhaps it is our dreams that settle it for us, and it depends on the book I have just read."

She was clad in a white flannel suit which delicately enveloped her in the floating softness of the material. Her bodice, with full folds, suggested, without displaying and without restraining, her free chest, which was firm and already ripe. And her superb neck emerged from a froth of soft lace, bending with gentle movements, fairer than her gown, a pilaster of flesh, bearing the heavy mass of her golden hair.

Servigny looked at her for a long time: "You are adorable this evening, Mam'zelle," said he, "I wish I could always see you like this."

"Don't make a declaration, Muscade. I should take it seriously, and that might cost you dear."

The Marquise seemed happy, very happy. All in black, richly dressed in a plain gown which showed her strong, full lines, a bit of red at the bodice, a cincture of red carnations falling from her waist like a chain, and fastened at the hips, and a red rose in her dark hair, she carried in all her person something fervid,—in that simple costume, in those flowers which seemed to bleed, in her look, in her slow speech, in her peculiar gestures.

Saval, too, appeared serious and absorbed. From time to time he stroked his pointed beard, trimmed in the fashion of Henri III., and seemed to be meditating on the most profound subjects.

Nobody spoke for several minutes. Then as they were serving the trout, Servigny remarked:

"Silence is a good thing, at times. People are often nearer to each other when they are keeping still than when they are talking. Isn't that so, Marquise?"

She turned a little toward him and answered:

"It is quite true. It is so sweet to think together about agreeable things."

She raised her warm glance toward Saval, and they continued for some seconds looking into each other's eyes. A slight, almost inaudible movement took place beneath the table.

Servigny resumed: "Mam'zelle Yvette, you will make me believe that you are in love if you keep on being as good as that. Now, with whom could you be in love? Let us think together, if you will; I put aside the army of vulgar sighers. I'll only take the principal ones. Is it Prince Kravalow?"

At this name Yvette awoke: "My poor Muscade, can you think of such a thing? Why, the Prince has the air of a Russian in a wax-figure museum, who has won medals in a hairdressing competition."

"Good! We'll drop the Prince. But you have noticed the Viscount Pierre de Belvigne?"

This time she began to laugh, and asked: "Can you imagine me hanging to the neck of 'Raisine'?" She nicknamed him according to the day, Raisine, Malvoisie, [Footnote: Preserved grapes and pears, malmsey,—a poor wine.] Argenteuil, for she gave everybody nicknames. And she would murmur to his face: "My dear little Pierre," or "My divine Pedro, darling Pierrot, give your bow-wow's head to your dear little girl, who wants to kiss it."

"Scratch out number two. There still remains the Chevalier Valreali whom the Marquise seems to favor," continued Servigny.

Yvette regained all her gaiety: "'Teardrop'? Why he weeps like a Magdalene. He goes to all the first-class funerals. I imagine myself dead every time he looks at me."

"That settles the third. So the lightning will strike Baron Saval, here."

"Monsieur the Colossus of Rhodes, Junior? No. He is too strong. It would seem to me as if I were in love with the triumphal arch of L'Etoile."

"Then Mam'zelle, it is beyond doubt that you are in love with me, for I am the only one of your adorers of whom we have not yet spoken. I left myself for the last through modesty and through discretion. It remains for me to thank you."

She replied with happy grace: "In love with you, Muscade? Ah! no. I like you, but I don't love you. Wait—I—I don't want to discourage you. I don't love you—yet. You have a chance—perhaps. Persevere, Muscade, be devoted, ardent, submissive, full of little attentions and considerations, docile to my slightest caprices, ready for anything to please me, and we shall see—later."

"But, Mam'zelle, I would rather furnish all you demand afterward than beforehand, if it be the same to you."

She asked with an artless air: "After what, Muscade?"

"After you have shown me that you love me, by Jove!"

"Well, act as if I loved you, and believe it, if you wish."

"But you—"

"Be quiet, Muscade; enough on the subject."

The sun had sunk behind the island, but the whole sky still flamed like a fire, and the peaceful water of the river seemed changed to blood. The reflections from the horizon reddened houses, objects, and persons. The scarlet rose in the Marquise's hair had the appearance of a splash of purple fallen from the clouds upon her head.

As Yvette looked on from her end, the Marquise rested, as if by carelessness, her bare hand upon Saval's hand; but the young girl made a motion and the Marquise withdrew her hand with a quick gesture, pretending to readjust something in the folds of her corsage.

Servigny, who was looking at them, said:

"If you like, Mam'zelle, we will take a walk on the island after dinner."

"Oh, yes! That will be delightful. We will go all alone, won't we, Muscade?"

"Yes, all alone, Mam'zelle!"

The vast silence of the horizon, the sleepy tranquillity of the evening captured heart, body, and voice. There are peaceful, chosen hours when it becomes almost impossible to talk.

The servants waited on them noiselessly. The firmamental conflagration faded away, and the soft night spread its shadows over the earth.

"Are you going to stay long in this place?" asked Saval.

And the Marquise answered, dwelling on each word: "Yes, as long as I am happy."

As it was too dark to see, lamps were brought. They cast upon the table a strange, pale gleam beneath the great obscurity of space; and very soon a shower of gnats fell upon the tablecloth—the tiny gnats which immolate themselves by passing over the glass chimneys, and, with wings and legs scorched, powder the table linen, dishes, and cups with a kind of gray and hopping dust.

They swallowed them in the wine, they ate them in the sauces, they saw them moving on the bread, and had their faces and hands tickled by the countless swarm of these tiny insects. They were continually compelled to throw away the beverages, to cover the plates, and while eating to shield the food with infinite precautions.

It amused Yvette. Servigny took care to shelter what she bore to her mouth, to guard her glass, to hold his handkerchief stretched out over her head like a roof. But the Marquise, disgusted, became nervous, and the end of the dinner came quickly. Yvette, who had not forgotten Servigny's proposition, said to him:

"Now we'll go to the island."

Her mother cautioned her in a languid tone: "Don't be late, above all things. We will escort you to the ferry."

And they started in couples, the young girl and her admirer walking in front, on the road to the shore. They heard, behind them, the Marquise and Saval speaking very rapidly in low tones. All was dark, with a thick, inky darkness. But the sky swarmed with grains of fire, and seemed to sow them in the river, for the black water was flecked with stars.

The frogs were croaking monotonously upon the bank, and numerous nightingales were uttering their low, sweet song in the calm and peaceful air.

Yvette suddenly said: "Gracious! They are not walking behind us any more, where are they?" And she called out: "Mamma!" No voice replied. The young girl resumed: "At any rate, they can't be far away, for I heard them just now."

Servigny murmured: "They must have gone back. Your mother was cold, perhaps." And he drew her along.

Before them a light gleamed. It was the tavern of Martinet, restaurant-keeper and fisherman. At their call a man came out of the house, and they got into a large boat which was moored among the weeds of the shore.

The ferryman took his oars, and the unwieldy barge, as it advanced, disturbed the sleeping stars upon the water and set them into a mad dance, which gradually calmed down after they had passed. They touched the other shore and disembarked beneath the great trees. A cool freshness of damp earth permeated the air under the lofty and clustered branches, where there seemed to be as many nightingales as there were leaves. A distant piano began to play a popular waltz.

Servigny took Yvette's arm and very gently slipped his hand around her waist and gave her a slight hug.

"What are you thinking about?" he said.

"I? About nothing at all. I am very happy!"

"Then you don't love me?"

"Oh, yes, Muscade, I love you, I love you a great deal; only leave me alone. It is too beautiful here to listen to your nonsense."

He drew her toward him, although she tried, by little pushes, to extricate herself, and through her soft flannel gown he felt the warmth of her flesh. He stammered:

"Yvette!"

"Well, what?"

"I do love you!"

"But you are not in earnest, Muscade."

"Oh, yes I am. I have loved you for a long time."

She continually kept trying to separate herself from him, trying to release the arm crushed between their bodies. They walked with difficulty, trammeled by this bond and by these movements, and went zigzagging along like drunken folk.

He knew not what to say to her, feeling that he could not talk to a young girl as he would to a woman. He was perplexed, thinking what he ought to do, wondering if she consented or did not understand, and curbing his spirit to find just the right, tender, and decisive words. He kept saying every second:

"Yvette! Speak! Yvette!"

Then, suddenly, risking all, he kissed her on the cheek. She gave a little start aside, and said with a vexed air:

"Oh! you are absurd. Are you going to let me alone?"

The tone of her voice did not at all reveal her thoughts nor her wishes; and, not seeing her too angry, he applied his lips to the beginning of her neck, just beneath the golden hair, that charming spot which he had so often coveted.

Then she made great efforts to free herself. But he held her strongly, and placing his other hand on her shoulder, he compelled her to turn her head toward him and gave her a fond, passionate kiss, squarely on the mouth.

She slipped from his arms by a quick undulation of the body, and, free from his grasp, she disappeared into the darkness with a great swishing of skirts, like the whir of a bird as it flies away.

He stood motionless a moment, surprised by her suppleness and her disappearance, then hearing nothing, he called gently: "Yvette!"

She did not reply. He began to walk forward, peering through the shadows, looking in the underbrush for the white spot her dress should make. All was dark. He cried out more loudly:

"Mam'zelle Yvette! Mam'zelle Yvette!"

Nothing stirred. He stopped and listened. The whole island was still; there was scarcely a rustle of leaves over his head. The frogs alone continued their deep croakings on the shores. Then he wandered from thicket to thicket, going where the banks were steep and bushy and returning to places where they were flat and bare as a dead man's arm. He proceeded until he was opposite Bougival and reached the establishment of La Grenouillere, groping the clumps of trees, calling out continually:

"Mam'zelle Yvette, where are you? Answer. It is ridiculous! Come, answer! Don't keep me hunting like this."

A distant clock began to strike. He counted the hours: twelve. He had been searching through the island for two hours. Then he thought that perhaps she had gone home; and he went back very anxiously, this time by way of the bridge. A servant dozing on a chair was waiting in the hall.

Servigny awakened him and asked: "Is it long since Mademoiselle Yvette came home? I left her at the foot of the place because I had a call to make."

And the valet replied: "Oh! yes, Monsieur, Mademoiselle came in before ten o'clock."

He proceeded to his room and went to bed. But he could not close his eyes. That stolen kiss had stirred him to the soul. He kept wondering what she thought and what she knew. How pretty and attractive she was!

His desires, somewhat wearied by the life he led, by all his procession of sweethearts, by all his explorations in the kingdom of love, awoke before this singular child, so fresh, irritating, and inexplicable. He heard one o'clock strike, then two. He could not sleep at all. He was warm, he felt his heart beat and his temples throb, and he rose to open the window. A breath of fresh air came in, which he inhaled deeply. The thick darkness was silent, black, motionless. But suddenly he perceived before him, in the shadows of the garden, a shining point; it seemed a little red coal.

"Well, a cigar!" he said to himself. "It must be Saval," and he called softly: "Leon!"

"Is it you, Jean?"

"Yes. Wait. I'll come down." He dressed, went out, and rejoining his friend who was smoking astride an iron chair, inquired: "What are you doing here at this hour?"

"I am resting," Saval replied. And he began to laugh. Servigny pressed his hand: "My compliments, my dear fellow. And as for me, I—am making a fool of myself."

"You mean—"

"I mean that—Yvette and her mother do not resemble each other."

"What has happened? Tell me."

Servigny recounted his attempts and their failure. Then he resumed:

"Decidedly, that little girl worries me. Fancy my not being able to sleep! What a queer thing a girl is! She appears to be as simple as anything, and yet you know nothing about her. A woman who has lived and loved, who knows life, can be quickly understood. But when it comes to a young virgin, on the contrary, no one can guess anything about her. At heart I begin to think that she is making sport of me."

Saval tilted his chair. He said, very slowly: "Take care, my dear fellow, she will lead you to marriage. Remember those other illustrious examples. It was just by this same process that Mademoiselle de Montijo, who was at least of good family, became empress. Don't play Napoleon."

Servigny murmured: "As for that, fear nothing. I am neither a simpleton nor an emperor. A man must be either one or the other to make such a move as that. But tell me, are you sleepy?"

"Not a bit."

"Will you take a walk along the river?"

"Gladly."

They opened the iron gate and began to walk along the river bank toward Marly. It was the quiet hour which precedes dawn, the hour of deep sleep, of complete rest, of profound peacefulness. Even the gentle sounds of the night were hushed. The nightingales sang no longer; the frogs had finished their hubbub; some kind of an animal only, probably a bird, was making somewhere a kind of sawing sound, feeble, monotonous, and regular as a machine. Servigny, who had moments of poetry, and of philosophy too, suddenly remarked: "Now this girl completely puzzles me. In arithmetic, one and one make two. In love one and one ought to make one but they make two just the same. Have you ever felt that? That need of absorbing a woman in yourself or disappearing in her? I am not speaking of the animal embrace, but of that moral and mental eagerness to be but one with a being, to open to her all one's heart and soul, and to fathom her thoughts to the depths."

"And yet you can never lay bare all the fluctuations of her wishes, desires, and opinions. You can never guess, even slightly, all the unknown currents, all the mystery of a soul that seems so near, a soul hidden behind two eyes that look at you, clear as water, transparent as if there were nothing beneath a soul which talks to you by a beloved mouth, which seems your very own, so greatly do you desire it; a soul which throws you by words its thoughts, one by one, and which, nevertheless, remains further away from you than those stars are from each other, and more impenetrable. Isn't it queer, all that?"

"I don't, ask so much," Saval rejoined. "I don't look behind the eyes. I care little for the contents, but much for the vessel." And Servigny replied: "What a singular person Yvette is! How will she receive me this morning?"

As they reached the works at Marly they perceived that the sky was brightening. The cocks began to crow in the poultry-yards. A bird twittered in a park at the left, ceaselessly reiterating a tender little theme.

"It is time to go back," said Saval.

They returned, and as Servigny entered his room, he saw the horizon all pink through his open windows.

Then he shut the blinds, drew the thick, heavy curtains, went back to bed and fell asleep. He dreamed of Yvette all through his slumber. An odd noise awoke him. He sat on the side of the bed and listened, but heard nothing further. Then suddenly there was a crackling against the blinds, like falling hail. He jumped from the bed, ran to the window, opened it, and saw Yvette standing in the path and throwing handfuls of gravel at his face. She was clad in pink, with a wide-brimmed straw hat ornamented with a mousquetaire plume, and was laughing mischievously.

"Well! Muscade, are you asleep? What could you have been doing all night to make you wake so late? Have you been seeking adventures, my poor Muscade?"

He was dazzled by the bright daylight striking him full in the eyes, still overwhelmed with fatigue, and surprised at the jesting tranquillity of the young girl.

"I'll be down in a second, Mam'zelle," he answered. "Just time to splash my face with water, and I will join you."

"Hurry," she cried, "it is ten o'clock, and besides I have a great plan to unfold to you, a plot we are going to concoct. You know that we breakfast at eleven."

He found her seated on a bench, with a book in her lap, some novel or other. She took his arm in a familiar and friendly way, with a frank and gay manner, as if nothing had happened the night before, and drew him toward the end of the garden.

"This is my plan," she said. "We will disobey mamma, and you shall take me presently to La Grenouillere restaurant. I want to see it. Mamma says that decent women cannot go to the place. Now it is all the same to me whether persons can go there or cannot. You'll take me, won't you, Muscade? And we will have a great time—with the boatmen."

She exhaled a delicious fragrance, although he could not exactly define just what light and vague odor enveloped her. It was not one of those heavy perfumes of her mother, but a discreet breath in which he fancied he could detect a suspicion of iris powder, and perhaps a suggestion of vervain.

Whence emanated that indiscernible perfume? From her dress, her hair, or her skin? He puzzled over this, and as he was speaking very close to her, he received full in the face her fresh breath, which seemed to him just as delicious to inhale.

Then he thought that this evasive perfume which he was trying to recognize was perhaps only evoked by her charming eyes, and was merely a sort of deceptive emanation of her young and alluring grace.

"That is agreed, isn't it, Muscade? As it will be very warm after breakfast, mamma will not go out. She always feels the heat very much. We will leave her with your friend, and you shall take me. They will think that we have gone into the forest. If you knew how much it will amuse me to see La Grenouillere!"

They reached the iron gate opposite the Seine. A flood of sunshine fell upon the slumberous, shining river. A slight heat-mist rose from it, a sort of haze of evaporated water, which spread over the surface of the stream a faint gleaming vapor.

From time to time, boats passed by, a quick yawl or a heavy passage boat, and short or long whistles could be heard, those of the trains which every Sunday poured the citizens of Paris into the suburbs, and those of the steamboats signaling their approach to pass the locks at Marly.

But a tiny bell sounded. Breakfast was announced, and they went back into the house. The repast was a silent one. A heavy July noon overwhelmed the earth, and oppressed humanity. The heat seemed thick, and paralyzed both mind and body. The sluggish words would not leave the lips, and all motion seemed laborious, as if the air had become a resisting medium, difficult to traverse. Only Yvette, although silent, seemed animated and nervous with impatience. As soon as they had finished the last course she said:

"If we were to go for a walk in the forest, it would be deliciously cool under the trees."

The Marquise murmured with a listless air: "Are you mad? Does anyone go out in such weather?"

And the young girl, delighted, rejoined: "Oh, well! We will leave the Baron to keep you company. Muscade and I will climb the hill and sit on the grass and read."

And turning toward Servigny she asked: "That is understood?"

"At your service, Mam'zelle," he replied.

Yvette ran to get her hat. The Marquise shrugged her shoulders with a sigh. "She certainly is mad." she said.

Then with an indolence in her amorous and lazy gestures, she gave her pretty white hand to the Baron, who kissed it softly. Yvette and Servigny started. They went along the river, crossed the bridge and went on to the island, and then seated themselves on the bank, beneath the willows, for it was too soon to go to La Grenouillere.

The young girl at once drew a book from her pocket and smilingly said: "Muscade, you are going to read to me." And she handed him the volume.

He made a motion as if of fright. "I, Mam'zelle? I don't know how to read!"

She replied with gravity: "Come, no excuses, no objections; you are a fine suitor, you! All for nothing, is that it? Is that your motto?"

He took the book, opened it, and was astonished. It was a treatise on entomology. A history of ants by an English author. And as he remained inert, believing that he was making sport of her, she said with impatience: "Well, read!"

"Is it a wager, or just a simple fad?" he asked.

"No, my dear. I saw that book in a shop. They told me that it was the best authority on ants and I thought that it would be interesting to learn about the life of these little insects while you see them running over the grass; so read, if you please."

She stretched herself flat upon the grass, her elbows resting upon the ground, her head between her hands, her eyes fixed upon the ground. He began to read as follows:

"The anthropoid apes are undoubtedly the animals which approach nearest to man by their anatomical structure, but if we consider the habits of the ants, their organization into societies, their vast communities, the houses and roads that they construct, their custom of domesticating animals, and sometimes even of making slaves of them, we are compelled to admit that they have the right to claim a place near to man in the scale of intelligence."

He continued in a monotonous voice, stopping from time to time to ask: "Isn't that enough?"

She shook her head, and having caught an ant on the end of a severed blade of grass, she amused herself by making it go from one end to the other of the sprig, which she tipped up whenever the insect reached one of the ends. She listened with mute and contented attention to all the wonderful details of the life of these frail creatures: their subterranean homes; the manner in which they seize, shut up, and feed plant-lice to drink the sweet milk which they secrete, as we keep cows in our barns; their custom of domesticating little blind insects which clean the anthills, and of going to war to capture slaves who will take care of their victors with such tender solicitude that the latter even lose the habit of feeding themselves.

And little by little, as if a maternal tenderness had sprung up in her heart for the poor insect which was so tiny and so intelligent, Yvette made it climb on her finger, looking at it with a moved expression, almost wanting to embrace it.

And as Servigny read of the way in which they live in communities, and play games of strength and skill among themselves, the young girl grew enthusiastic and sought to kiss the insect which escaped her and began to crawl over her face. Then she uttered a piercing cry, as if she had been threatened by a terrible danger, and with frantic gestures tried to brush it off her face. With a loud laugh Servigny caught it near her tresses and imprinted on the spot where he had seized it a long kiss without Yvette withdrawing her forehead.

Then she exclaimed as she rose: "That is better than a novel. Now let us go to La Grenouillere."

They reached that part of the island which is set out as a park and shaded with great trees. Couples were strolling beneath the lofty foliage along the Seine, where the boats were gliding by.

The boats were filled with young people, working-girls and their sweethearts, the latter in their shirt-sleeves, with coats on their arms, tall hats tipped back, and a jaded look. There were tradesmen with their families, the women dressed in their best and the children flocking like little chicks about their parents. A distant, continuous sound of voices, a heavy, scolding clamor announced the proximity of the establishment so dear to the boatmen.

Suddenly they saw it. It was a huge boat, roofed over, moored to the bank. On board were many men and women drinking at tables, or else standing up, shouting, singing, bandying words, dancing, capering, to the sound of a piano which was groaning—out of tune and rattling as an old kettle.

Two tall, russet-haired, half-tipsy girls, with red lips, were talking coarsely. Others were dancing madly with young fellows half clad, dressed like jockeys, in linen trousers and colored caps. The odors of a crowd and of rice-powder were noticeable.

The drinkers around the tables were swallowing white, red, yellow, and green liquids, and vociferating at the top of their lungs, feeling as it were, the necessity of making a noise, a brutal need of having their ears and brains filled with uproar. Now and then a swimmer, standing on the roof, dived into the water, splashing the nearest guests, who yelled like savages.

On the stream passed the flotillas of light craft, long, slender wherries, swiftly rowed by bare-armed oarsmen, whose muscles played beneath their bronzed skin. The women in the boats, in blue or red flannel skirts, with umbrellas, red or blue, opened over their heads and gleaming under the burning sun, leaned back in their chairs at the stern of the boats, and seemed almost to float upon the water, in motionless and slumberous pose.

The heavier boats proceeded slowly, crowded with people. A collegian, wanting to show off, rowed like a windmill against all the other boats, bringing the curses of their oarsmen down upon his head, and disappearing in dismay after almost drowning two swimmers, followed by the shouts of the crowd thronging in the great floating cafe.

Yvette, radiantly happy, taking Servigny's arm, went into the midst of this noisy mob. She seemed to enjoy the crowding, and stared at the girls with a calm and gracious glance.

"Look at that one, Muscade," she said. "What pretty hair she has! They seem to be having such fun!"

As the pianist, a boatman dressed in red with a huge straw hat, began a waltz, Yvette grasped her companion and they danced so long and madly that everybody looked at them. The guests, standing on the tables, kept time with their feet; others threw glasses, and the musician, seeming to go mad, struck the ivory keys with great bangs; swaying his whole body and swinging his head covered with that immense hat. Suddenly he stopped and, slipping to the deck, lay flat, beneath his head-gear, as if dead with fatigue. A loud laugh arose and everybody applauded.

Four friends rushed forward, as they do in cases of accident, and lifting up their comrade, they carried him by his four limbs, after carefully placing his great hat on his stomach. A joker following them intoned the "De Profundis," and a procession formed and threaded the paths of the island, guests and strollers and everyone they met falling into line.

Yvette darted forward, delighted, laughing with her whole heart, chatting with everybody, stirred by the movement and the noise. The young men gazed at her, crowded against her, seeming to devour her with their glances; and Servigny began to fear lest the adventure should terminate badly.

The procession still kept on its way; hastening its step; for the four bearers had taken a quick pace, followed by the yelling crowd. But suddenly, they turned toward the shore, stopped short as they reached the bank, swung their comrade for a moment, and then, all four acting together, flung him into the river.

A great shout of joy rang out from all mouths, while the poor pianist, bewildered, paddled, swore, coughed, and spluttered, and though sticking in the mud managed to get to the shore. His hat which floated down the stream was picked up by a boat. Yvette danced with joy, clapping and repeating: "Oh! Muscade, what fun! what fun!"

Servigny looked on, having become serious, a little disturbed, a little chilled to see her so much at her ease in this common place. A sort of instinct revolted in him, that instinct of the proper, which a well-born man always preserves even when he casts himself loose, that instinct which avoids too common familiarities and too degrading contacts. Astonished, he muttered to himself:

"Egad! Then YOU are at home here, are you?" And he wanted to speak familiarly to her, as a man does to certain women the first time he meets them. He no longer distinguished her from the russet-haired, hoarse-voiced creatures who brushed against them. The language of the crowd was not at all choice, but nobody seemed shocked or surprised. Yvette did not even appear to notice it.

"Muscade, I want to go in bathing," she said. "We'll go into the river together."

"At your service," said he.

They went to the bath-office to get bathing-suits. She was ready the first, and stood on the bank waiting for him, smiling on everyone who looked at her. Then side by side they went into the luke-warm water.

She swam with pleasure, with intoxication, caressed by the wave, throbbing with a sensual delight, raising herself at each stroke as if she were going to spring from the water. He followed her with difficulty, breathless, and vexed to feel himself mediocre at the sport.

But she slackened her pace, and then, turning over suddenly, she floated, with her arms folded and her eyes wide open to the blue sky. He observed, thus stretched out on the surface of the river, the undulating lines of her form, her firm neck and shoulders, her slightly submerged hips, and bare ankles, gleaming in the water, and the tiny foot that emerged.

He saw her thus exhibiting herself, as if she were doing it on purpose, to lure him on, or again to make sport of him. And he began to long for her with a passionate ardor and an exasperating impatience. Suddenly she turned, looked at him, and burst into laughter.

"You have a fine head," she said.

He was annoyed at this bantering, possessed with the anger of a baffled lover. Then yielding brusquely to a half felt desire for retaliation, a desire to avenge himself, to wound her, he said:

"Well, does this sort of life suit you?"

She asked with an artless air: "What do you mean?"

"Oh, come, don't make game of me. You know well enough what I mean!"

"No, I don't, on my word of honor."

"Oh, let us stop this comedy! Will you or will you not?"

"I do not understand you."

"You are not as stupid as all that; besides I told you last night."

"Told me what? I have forgotten!"

"That I love you."

"You?"

"Yes."

"What nonsense!"

"I swear it."

"Then prove it."

"That is all I ask."

"What is?"

"To prove it."

"Well, do so."

"But you did not say so last night."

"You did not ask anything."

"What absurdity!"

"And besides it is not to me to whom you should make your proposition."

"To whom, then?"

"Why, to mamma, of course."

He burst into laughter. "To your mother. No, that is too much!"

She had suddenly become very grave, and looking him straight in the eyes, said:

"Listen, Muscade, if you really love me enough to marry me, speak to mamma first, and I will answer you afterward."

He thought she was still making sport of him, and angrily replied: "Mam'zelle, you must be taking me for somebody else."

She kept looking at him with her soft, clear eyes. She hesitated and then said:

"I don't understand you at all."

Then he answered quickly with somewhat of ill nature in his voice:

"Come now, Yvette, let us cease this absurd comedy, which has already lasted too long. You are playing the part of a simple little girl, and the role does not fit you at all, believe me. You know perfectly well that there can be no question of marriage between us, but merely of love. I have told you that I love you. It is the truth. I repeat, I love you. Don't pretend any longer not to understand me, and don't treat me as if I were a fool."

They were face to face, treading water, merely moving their hands a little, to steady themselves. She was still for a moment, as if she could not make out the meaning of his words, then she suddenly blushed up to the roots of her hair. Her whole face grew purple from her neck to her ears, which became almost violet, and without answering a word she fled toward the shore, swimming with all her strength with hasty strokes. He could not keep up with her and panted with fatigue as he followed. He saw her leave the water, pick up her cloak, and go to her dressing-room without looking back.

It took him a long time to dress, very much perplexed as to what he ought to do, puzzled over what he should say to her, and wondering whether he ought to excuse himself or persevere. When he was ready, she had gone away all alone. He went back slowly, anxious and disturbed.

The Marquise was strolling, on Saval's arm, in the circular path around the lawn. As she observed Servigny, she said, with that careless air which she had maintained since the night before.

"I told you not to go out in such hot weather. And now Yvette has come back almost with a sun stroke. She has gone to lie down. She was as red as a poppy, the poor child, and she has a frightful headache. You must have been walking in the full sunlight, or you must have done something foolish. You are as unreasonable as she."

The young girl did not come down to dinner. When they wanted to send her up something to eat she called through the door that she was not hungry, for she had shut herself in, and she begged that they would leave her undisturbed. The two young men left by the ten o'clock train, promising to return the following Thursday, and the Marquise seated herself at the open window to dream, hearing in the distance the orchestra of the boatmen's ball, with its sprightly music, in the deep and solemn silence of the night.

Swayed by love as a person is moved by a fondness for horses or boating, she was subject to sudden tendernesses which crept over her like a disease. These passions took possession of her suddenly, penetrated her entire being, maddened her, enervated or overwhelmed her, in measure as they were of an exalted, violent, dramatic, or sentimental character.

She was one of those women who are created to love and to be loved. Starting from a very low station in life, she had risen in her adventurous career, acting instinctively, with inborn cleverness, accepting money and kisses, naturally, without distinguishing between them, employing her extraordinary ability in an unthinking and simple fashion. From all her experiences she had never known either a genuine tenderness or a great repulsion.

She had had various friends, for she had to live, as in traveling a person eats at many tables. But occasionally her heart took fire, and she really fell in love, which state lasted for some weeks or months, according to conditions. These were the delicious moments of her life, for she loved with all her soul. She cast herself upon love as a person throws himself into the river to drown himself, and let herself be carried away, ready to die, if need be, intoxicated, maddened, infinitely happy. She imagined each time that she never had experienced anything like such an attachment, and she would have been greatly astonished if some one had told her of how many men she had dreamed whole nights through, looking at the stars.

Saval had captivated her, body and soul. She dreamed of him, lulled by his face and his memory, in the calm exaltation of consummated love, of present and certain happiness.

A sound behind her made her turn around. Yvette had just entered, still in her daytime dress, but pale, with eyes glittering, as sometimes is the case after some great fatigue. She leaned on the sill of the open window, facing her mother.

"I want to speak to you," she said.

The Marquise looked at her in astonishment. She loved her like an egotistical mother, proud of her beauty, as a person is proud of a fortune, too pretty still herself to become jealous, too indifferent to plan the schemes with which they charged her, too clever, nevertheless, not to have full consciousness of her daughter's value.

"I am listening, my child," she said; "what is it?"

Yvette gave her a piercing look, as if to read the depths of her soul and to seize all the sensations which her words might awake.

"It is this. Something strange has just happened."

"What can it be?"

"Monsieur de Servigny has told me that he loves me."

The Marquise, disturbed, waited a moment, and, as Yvette said nothing more, she asked:

"How did he tell you that? Explain yourself!"

Then the young girl, sitting at her mother's feet, in a coaxing attitude common with her, and clasping her hands, added:

"He asked me to marry him."

Madame Obardi made a sudden gesture of stupefaction and cried:

"Servigny! Why! you are crazy!"

Yvette had not taken her eyes off her mother's face, watching her thoughts and her surprise. She asked with a serious voice:

"Why am I crazy? Why should not Monsieur de Servigny marry me?"

The Marquise, embarrassed, stammered:

"You are mistaken, it is not possible. You either did not hear or did not understand. Monsieur de Servigny is too rich for you, and too much of a Parisian to marry." Yvette rose softly. She added: "But if he loves me as he says he does, mamma?"

Her mother replied, with some impatience: "I thought you big enough and wise enough not to have such ideas. Servigny is a man-about-town and an egotist. He will never marry anyone but a woman of his set and his fortune. If he asked you in marriage, it is only that he wants—"

The Marquise, incapable of expressing her meaning, was silent for a moment, then continued: "Come now, leave me alone and go to bed."

And the young girl, as if she had learned what she sought to find out, answered in a docile voice: "Yes, mamma!"

She kissed her mother on the forehead and withdrew with a calm step. As she reached the door, the Marquise called out: "And your sunstroke?" she said.

"I did not have one at all. It was that which caused everything."

The Marquise added: "We will not speak of it again. Only don't stay alone with him for some time from now, and be very sure that he will never marry you, do you understand, and that he merely means to—compromise you."

She could not find better words to express her thought. Yvette went to her room. Madame Obardi began to dream. Living for years in an opulent and loving repose, she had carefully put aside all reflections which might annoy or sadden her. Never had she been willing to ask herself the question.—What would become of Yvette? It would be soon enough to think about the difficulties when they arrived. She well knew, from her experience, that her daughter could not marry a man who was rich and of good society, excepting by a totally improbable chance, by one of those surprises of love which place adventuresses on thrones.

She had not considered it, furthermore, being too much occupied with herself to make any plans which did not directly concern herself.

Yvette would do as her mother, undoubtedly. She would lead a gay life. Why not? But the Marquise had never dared ask when, or how. That would all come about in time.

And now her daughter, all of a sudden, without warning, had asked one of those questions which could not be answered, forcing her to take an attitude in an affair, so delicate, so dangerous in every respect, and so disturbing to the conscience which a woman is expected to show in matters concerning her daughter.

Sometimes nodding but never asleep, she had too much natural astuteness to be deceived a minute about Servigny's intentions, for she knew men by experience, and especially men of that set. So at the first words uttered by Yvette, she had cried almost in spite of herself: "Servigny, marry you? You are crazy!"

How had he come to employ that old method, he, that sharp man of the world? What would he do now? And she, the young girl, how should she warn her more clearly and even forbid her, for she might make great mistakes. Would anyone have believed that this big girl had remained so artless, so ill informed, so guileless? And the Marquise, greatly perplexed and already wearied with her reflections, endeavored to make up her mind what to do without finding a solution of the problem, for the situation seemed to her very embarrassing. Worn out with this worry, she thought:

"I will watch them more clearly, I will act according to circumstances. If necessary, I will speak to Servigny, who is sharp and will take a hint."

She did not think out what she should say to him, nor what he would answer, nor what sort of an understanding could be established between them, but happy at being relieved of this care without having had to make a decision, she resumed her dreams of the handsome Saval, and turning toward that misty light which hovers over Paris, she threw kisses with both hands toward the great city, rapid kisses which she tossed into the darkness, one after the other, without counting; and, very low, as if she were talking to Saval still, she murmured:

"I love you, I love you!"

CHAPTER III
ENLIGHTENMENT

Yvette, also, could not sleep. Like her mother, she leaned upon the sill of the open window, and tears, her first bitter tears, filled her eyes. Up to this time she had lived, had grown up, in the heedless and serene confidence of happy youth. Why should she have dreamed, reflected, puzzled? Why should she not have been a young girl, like all other young girls? Why should a doubt, a fear, or painful suspicion have come to her?

She seemed posted on all topics because she had a way of talking on all subjects, because she had taken the tone, demeanor, and words of the people who lived around her. But she really knew no more than a little girl raised in a convent; her audacities of speech came from her memory, from that unconscious faculty of imitation and assimilation which women possess, and not from a mind instructed and emboldened.

She spoke of love as the son of a painter or a musician would, at the age of ten or twelve years, speak of painting or music. She knew or rather suspected very well what sort of mystery this word concealed;—too many jokes had been whispered before her, for her innocence not to be a trifle enlightened,—but how could she have drawn the conclusion from all this, that all families did not resemble hers?

They kissed her mother's hand with the semblance of respect; all their friends had titles; they all were rich or seemed to be so; they all spoke familiarly of the princes of the royal line. Two sons of kings had even come often, in the evening, to the Marquise's house. How should she have known?

And, then, she was naturally artless. She did not estimate or sum up people as her mother, did. She lived tranquilly, too joyous in her life to worry herself about what might appear suspicious to creatures more calm, thoughtful, reserved, less cordial, and sunny.

But now, all at once, Servigny, by a few words, the brutality of which she felt without understanding them, awakened in her a sudden disquietude, unreasoning at first, but which grew into a tormenting apprehension. She had fled home, had escaped like a wounded animal, wounded in fact most deeply by those words which she ceaselessly repeated to get all their sense and bearing: "You know very well that there can be no question of marriage between us—but only of love."

What did he mean? And why this insult? Was she then in ignorance of something, some secret, some shame? She was the only one ignorant of it, no doubt. But what could she do? She was frightened, startled, as a person is when he discovers some hidden infamy, some treason of a beloved friend, one of those heart-disasters which crush.

She dreamed, reflected, puzzled, wept, consumed by fears and suspicions. Then her joyous young soul reassuring itself, she began to plan an adventure, to imagine an abnormal and dramatic situation, founded on the recollections of all the poetical romances she had read. She recalled all the moving catastrophes, or sad and touching stories; she jumbled them together, and concocted a story of her own with which she interpreted the half-understood mystery which enveloped her life.

She was no longer cast down. She dreamed, she lifted veils, she imagined unlikely complications, a thousand singular, terrible things, seductive, nevertheless, by their very strangeness. Could she be, by chance, the natural daughter of a prince? Had her poor mother, betrayed and deserted, made Marquise by some king, perhaps King Victor Emmanuel, been obliged to take flight before the anger of the family? Was she not rather a child abandoned by its relations, who were noble and illustrious, the fruit of a clandestine love, taken in by the Marquise, who had adopted and brought her up?

Still other suppositions passed through her mind. She accepted or rejected them according to the dictates of her fancy. She was moved to pity over her own case, happy at the bottom of her heart, and sad also, taking a sort of satisfaction in becoming a sort of a heroine of a book who must: assume a noble attitude, worthy of herself.

She laid out the part she must play, according to events at which she guessed. She vaguely outlined this role, like one of Scribe's or of George Sand's. It should be endued with devotion, self-abnegation, greatness of soul, tenderness; and fine words. Her pliant nature almost rejoiced in this new attitude. She pondered almost till evening what she should do, wondering how she should manage to wrest the truth from the Marquise.

And when night came, favorable to tragic situations, she had thought out a simple and subtile trick to obtain what she wanted: it was, brusquely, to say that Servigny had asked for her hand in marriage.

At this news, Madame Obardi, taken by surprise, would certainly let a word escape her lips, a cry which would throw light into the mind of her daughter. And Yvette had accomplished her plan.

She expected an explosion of astonishment, an expansion of love, a confidence full of gestures and tears. But, instead of this, her mother, without appearing stupefied or grieved, had only seemed bored; and from the constrained, discontented, and worried tone in which she had replied, the young girl, in whom there suddenly awaked all the astuteness, keenness, and sharpness of a woman, understanding that she must not insist, that the mystery was of another nature, that it would be painful to her to learn it, and that she must puzzle it out all alone, had gone back to her room, her heart oppressed, her soul in distress, possessed now with the apprehensions of a real misfortune, without knowing exactly either whence or why this emotion came to her. So she wept, leaning at the window.

She wept long, not dreaming of anything now, not seeking to discover anything more, and little by little, weariness overcoming her, she closed her eyes. She dozed for a few minutes, with that deep sleep of people who are tired out and have not the energy to undress and go to bed, that heavy sleep, broken by dreams, when the head nods upon the breast.

She did not go to bed until the first break of day, when the cold of the morning, chilling her, compelled her to leave the window.

The next day and the day after, she maintained a reserved and melancholy attitude. Her thoughts were busy; she was learning to spy out, to guess at conclusions, to reason. A light, still vague, seemed to illumine men and things around her in a new manner; she began to entertain suspicions against all, against everything that she had believed, against her mother. She imagined all sorts of things during these two days. She considered all the possibilities, taking the most extreme resolutions with the suddenness of her changeable and unrestrained nature. Wednesday she hit upon a plan, an entire schedule of conduct and a system of spying. She rose Thursday morning with the resolve to be very sharp and armed against everybody.

She determined even to take for her motto these two words: "Myself alone," and she pondered for more than an hour how she should arrange them to produce a good effect engraved about her crest, on her writing paper.

Saval and Servigny arrived at ten o'clock. The young girl gave her hand with reserve, without embarrassment, and in a tone, familiar though grave, she said:

"Good morning, Muscade, are you well?" "Good morning, Mam'zelle, fairly, thanks, and you?" He was watching her. "What comedy will she play me," he said to himself.

The Marquise having taken Saval's arm, he took Yvette's, and they began to stroll about the lawn, appearing and disappearing every minute, behind the clumps of trees.

Yvette walked with a thoughtful air, looking at the gravel of the pathway, appearing hardly to hear what her companion said and scarcely answering him.

Suddenly she asked: "Are you truly my friend, Muscade?"

"Why, of course, Mam'zelle."

"But truly, truly, now?"

"Absolutely your friend, Mam'zelle, body and soul."

"Even enough of a friend not to lie to me once, just once?"

"Even twice, if necessary."

"Even enough to tell me the absolute, exact truth?"

"Yes, Mam'zelle."

"Well, what do you think, way down in your heart, of the Prince of Kravalow?"

"Ah, the devil!"

"You see that you are already preparing to lie."

"Not at all, but I am seeking the words, the proper words. Great Heavens, Prince Kravalow is a Russian, who speaks Russian, who was born in Russia, who has perhaps had a passport to come to France, and about whom there is nothing false but his name and title."

She looked him in the eyes: "You mean that he is—?"

"An adventurer, Mam'zelle."

"Thank you, and Chevalier Valreali is no better?" "You have hit it."

"And Monsieur de Belvigne?"

"With him it is a different thing. He is of provincial society, honorable up to a certain point, but only a little scorched from having lived too rapidly."

"And you?"

"I am what they call a butterfly, a man of good family, who had intelligence and who has squandered it in making phrases, who had good health and who has injured it by dissipation, who had some worth perhaps and who has scattered it by doing nothing. There is left to me a certain knowledge of life, a complete absence of prejudice, a large contempt for mankind, including women, a very deep sentiment of the uselessness of my acts and a vast tolerance for the mob."

"Nevertheless, at times, I can be frank, and I am even capable of affection, as you could see, if you would. With these defects and qualities I place myself at your orders, Mam'zelle, morally and physically, to do what you please with me."

She did not laugh; she listened, weighing his words and his intentions; then she resumed:

"What do you think of the Countess de Lammy?"

He replied, vivaciously: "You will permit me not to give my opinion about the women."

"About none of them?"

"About none of them." "Then you must have a bad opinion of them all. Come, think; won't you make a single exception?"

He sneered with that insolent air which he generally wore; and with that brutal audacity which he used as a weapon, he said: "Present company is always excepted."

She blushed a little, but calmly asked: "Well, what do you think of me?"

"You want me to tell. Well, so be it. I think you are a young person of good sense, and practicalness, or if you prefer, of good practical sense, who knows very well how to arrange her pastime, to amuse people, to hide her views, to lay her snares, and who, without hurrying, awaits events."

"Is that all?" she asked.

"That's all."

Then she said with a serious earnestness: "I shall make you change that opinion, Muscade."

Then she joined her mother, who was proceeding with short steps, her head down, with that manner assumed in talking very low, while walking, of very intimate and very sweet things. As she advanced she drew shapes in the sand, letters perhaps, with the point of her sunshade, and she spoke, without looking at Saval, long, softly, leaning on his arm, pressed against him.

Yvette suddenly fixed her eyes upon her, and a suspicion, rather a feeling than a doubt, passed through her mind as a shadow of a cloud driven by the wind passes over the ground.

The bell rang for breakfast. It was silent and almost gloomy. There was a storm in the air. Great solid clouds rested upon the horizon, mute and heavy, but charged with a tempest. As soon as they had taken their coffee on the terrace, the Marquise asked:

"Well, darling, are you going to take a walk today with your friend Servigny? It is a good time to enjoy the coolness under the trees."

Yvette gave her a quick glance.

"No, mamma, I am not going out to-day."

The Marquise appeared annoyed, and insisted. "Oh, go and take a stroll, my child, it is excellent for you."

Then Yvette distinctly said: "No, mamma, I shall stay in the house to-day, and you know very well why, because I told you the other evening."

Madame Obardi gave it no further thought, preoccupied with the thought of remaining alone with Saval. She blushed and was annoyed, disturbed on her own account, not knowing how she could find a free hour or two. She stammered:

"It is true. I was not thinking of it. I don't know where my head is."

And Yvette taking up some embroidery, which she called "the public safety," and at which she worked five or six times a year, on dull days, seated herself on a low chair near her mother, while the two young men, astride folding-chairs, smoked their cigars.

The hours passed in a languid conversation. The Marquise fidgety, cast longing glances at Saval, seeking some pretext, some means, of getting rid of her daughter. She finally realized that she would not succeed, and not knowing what ruse to employ, she said to Servigny: "You know, my dear Duke, that I am going to keep you both this evening. To-morrow we shall breakfast at the Fournaise restaurant, at Chaton."

He understood, smiled, and bowed: "I am at your orders, Marquise."

The day wore on slowly and painfully under the threatenings of the storm. The hour for dinner gradually approached. The heavy sky was filled with slow and heavy clouds. There was not a breath of air stirring. The evening meal was silent, too. An oppression, an embarrassment, a sort of vague fear, seemed to make the two men and the two women mute.

When the covers were removed, they sat long upon the terrace; only speaking at long intervals. Night fell, a sultry night. Suddenly the horizon was torn by an immense flash of lightning, which illumined with a dazzling and wan light the four faces shrouded in darkness. Then a far-off sound, heavy and feeble, like the rumbling of a carriage upon a bridge, passed over the earth; and it seemed that the heat of the atmosphere increased, that the air suddenly became more oppressive, and the silence of the evening deeper.

Yvette rose. "I am going to bed," she said, "the storm makes me ill."

And she offered her brow to the Marquise, gave her hand to the two young men, and withdrew.

As her room was just above the terrace, the leaves of a great chestnut-tree growing before the door soon gleamed with a green hue, and Servigny kept his eyes fixed on this pale light in the foliage, in which at times he thought he saw a shadow pass. But suddenly the light went out. Madame Obardi gave a great sigh.

"My daughter has gone to bed," she said.

Servigny rose, saying: "I am going to do as much, Marquise, if you will permit me." He kissed the hand she held out to him and disappeared in turn.

She was left alone with Saval, in the night. In a moment she was clasped in his arms. Then, although he tried to prevent her, she kneeled before him murmuring: "I want to see you by the lightning flashes."

But Yvette, her candle snuffed out, had returned to her balcony, barefoot, gliding like a shadow, and she listened, consumed by an unhappy and confused suspicion. She could not see, as she was above them, on the roof of the terrace.

She heard nothing but a murmur of voices, and her heart beat so fast that she could actually hear its throbbing. A window closed on the floor above her. Servigny, then, must have just gone up to his room. Her mother was alone with the other man.

A second flash of lightning, clearing the sky; lighted up for a second all the landscape she knew so well, with a startling and sinister gleam, and she saw the great river, with the color of melted lead, as a river appears in dreams in fantastic scenes.

Just then a voice below her uttered the words: "I love you!" And she heard nothing more. A strange shudder passed over her body, and her soul shivered in frightful distress. A heavy, infinite silence, which seemed eternal, hung over the world. She could no longer breathe, her breast oppressed by something unknown and horrible. Another flash of lightning illumined space, lighting up the horizon for an instant, then another almost immediately came, followed by still others. And the voice, which she had already heard, repeated more loudly: "Oh! how I love you! how I love you!" And Yvette recognized the voice; it was her mother's.

A large drop of warm rain fell upon her brow, and a slight and almost imperceptible motion ran through the leaves, the quivering of the rain which was now beginning. Then a noise came from afar, a confused sound, like that of the wind in the branches: it was the deluge descending in sheets on earth and river and trees. In a few minutes the water poured about her, covering her, drenching her like a shower-bath. She did not move, thinking only of what was happening on the terrace.

She heard them get up and go to their rooms. Doors were closed within the house; and the young girl, yielding to an irresistible desire to learn what was going on, a desire which maddened and tortured her, glided downstairs, softly opened the outer door, and, crossing the lawn under the furious downpour, ran and hid in a clump of trees, to look at the windows.

Only one window was lighted, her mother's. And suddenly two shadows appeared in the luminous square, two shadows, side by side. Then distracted, without reflection, without knowing what she was doing, she screamed with all her might, in a shrill voice: "Mamma!" as a person would cry out to warn people in danger of death.

Her desperate cry was lost in the noise of the rain, but the couple separated, disturbed. And one of the shadows disappeared, while the other tried to discover something, peering through the darkness of the garden.

Fearing to be surprised, or to meet her mother at that moment, Yvette rushed back to the house, ran upstairs, dripping wet, and shut herself in her room, resolved to open her door to no one.

Without taking, off her streaming dress, which clung to her form, she fell on her knees, with clasped hands, in her distress imploring some superhuman protection, the mysterious aid of Heaven, the unknown support which a person seeks in hours of tears and despair.

The great lightning flashes threw for an instant their livid reflections into her room, and she saw herself in the mirror of her wardrobe, with her wet and disheveled hair, looking so strange that she did not recognize herself. She remained there so long that the storm abated without her perceiving it. The rain ceased, a light filled the sky, still obscured with clouds, and a mild, balmy, delicious freshness, a freshness of grass and wet leaves, came in through the open window.

Yvette rose, took off her wet, cold garments, without thinking what she was doing, and went to bed. She stared with fixed eyes at the dawning day. Then she wept again, and then she began to think.

Her mother! A lover! What a shame! She had read so many books in which women, even mothers, had overstepped the bounds of propriety, to regain their honor at the pages of the climax, that she was not astonished beyond measure at finding herself enveloped in a drama similar to all those of her reading. The violence of her first grief, the cruel shock of surprise, had already worn off a little, in the confused remembrance of analogous situations. Her mind had rambled among such tragic adventures, painted by the novel-writers, that the horrible discovery seemed, little by little, like the natural continuation of some serial story, begun the evening before.

She said to herself: "I will save my mother." And almost reassured by this heroic resolution, she felt herself strengthened, ready at once for the devotion and the struggle. She reflected on the means which must be employed. A single one seemed good, which was quite in keeping with her romantic nature. And she rehearsed the interview which she should have with the Marquise, as an actor rehearses the scene which he is going to play.

The sun had risen. The servants were stirring about the house. The chambermaid came with the chocolate. Yvette put the tray on the table and said:

"You will say to my mother that I am not well, that I am going to stay in bed until those gentlemen leave, that I could not sleep last night, and that I do not want to be disturbed because I am going to try to rest."

The servant, surprised, looked at the wet dress, which had fallen like a rag on the carpet.

"So Mademoiselle has been out?" she said.

"Yes, I went out for a walk in the rain to refresh myself."

The maid picked up the skirts, stockings, and wet shoes; then she went away carrying on her arm, with fastidious precautions, these garments, soaked as the clothes of a drowned person. And Yvette waited, well knowing that her mother would come to her.

The Marquise entered, having jumped from her bed at the first words of the chambermaid, for a suspicion had possessed her, heart since that cry: "Mamma!" heard in the dark.

"What is the matter?" she said.

Yvette looked at her and stammered: "I—I—" Then overpowered by a sudden and terrible emotion, she began to choke.

The Marquise, astonished, again asked: "What in the world is the matter with you?"

Then, forgetting all her plans and prepared phrases, the young girl hid her face in both hands and stammered:

"Oh! mamma! Oh! mamma!"

Madame Obardi stood by the bed, too much affected thoroughly to understand, but guessing almost everything, with that subtile instinct whence she derived her strength. As Yvette could not speak, choked with tears, her mother, worn out finally and feeling some fearful explanation coming, brusquely asked:

"Come, will you tell me what the matter is?"

Yvette could hardly utter the words: "Oh! last night—I saw—your window."

The Marquise, very pale; said: "Well? what of it?"

Her daughter repeated, still sobbing: "Oh! mamma! Oh! mamma!"

Madame Obardi, whose fear and embarrassment turned to anger, shrugged her shoulders and turned to go. "I really believe that you are crazy. When this ends, you will let me know."

But the young girl, suddenly took her hands from her face, which was streaming with tears.

"No, listen, I must speak to you, listen. You must promise me—we must both go, away, very far off, into the country, and we must live like the country people; and no one must know what has become of us. Say you will, mamma; I beg you, I implore you; will you?"

The Marquise, confused, stood in the middle of the room. She had in her veins the irascible blood of the common people. Then a sense of shame, a mother's modesty, mingled with a vague sentiment of fear and the exasperation of a passionate woman whose love is threatened, and she shuddered, ready to ask for pardon, or to yield to some violence.

"I don't understand you," she said.

Yvette replied:

"I saw you, mamma, last night. You cannot—if you knew—we will both go away. I will love you so much that you will forget—"

Madame Obardi said in a trembling voice: "Listen, my daughter, there are some things which you do not yet understand. Well, don't forget—don't forget-that I forbid you ever to speak to me about those things."

But the young girl, brusquely taking the role of savior which she had imposed upon herself, rejoined:

"No, mamma, I am no longer a child, and I have the right to know. I know that we receive persons of bad repute, adventurers, and I know that, on that account, people do not respect us. I know more. Well, it must not be, any longer, do you hear? I do not wish it. We will go away: you will sell your jewels; we will work, if need be, and we will live as honest women, somewhere very far away. And if I can marry, so much the better."

She answered: "You are crazy. You will do me the favor to rise and come down to breakfast with all the rest."

"No, mamma. There is some one whom I shall never see again, you understand me. I want him to leave, or I shall leave. You shall choose between him and me."

She was sitting up in bed, and she raised her voice, speaking as they do on the stage, playing, finally, the drama which she had dreamed, almost forgetting her grief in the effort to fulfill her mission.

The Marquise, stupefied, again repeated: "You are crazy—" not finding anything else to say.

Yvette replied with a theatrical energy: "No, mamma, that man shall leave the house, or I shall go myself, for I will not weaken."

"And where will you go? What will you do?"

"I do not know, it matters little—I want you to be an honest woman."

These words which recurred, aroused in the Marquise a perfect fury, and she cried:

"Be silent. I do not permit you to talk to me like that. I am as good as anybody else, do you understand? I lead a certain sort of life, it is true, and I am proud of it; the 'honest women' are not as good as I am."

Yvette, astonished, looked at her, and stammered: "Oh! mamma!"

But the Marquise, carried away with excitement, continued:

"Yes, I lead a certain life—what of it? Otherwise you would be a cook, as I was once, and earn thirty sous a day. You would be washing dishes, and your mistress would send you to market—do you understand—and she would turn you out if you loitered, just as you loiter, now because I am—because I lead this life. Listen. When a person is only a nursemaid, a poor girl, with fifty francs saved up, she must know how to manage, if she does not want to starve to death; and there are not two ways for us, there are not two ways, do you understand, when we are servants. We cannot make our fortune with official positions, nor with stockjobbing tricks. We have only one way—only one way."

She struck her breast as a penitent at the confessional, and flushed and excited, coming toward the bed, she continued: "So much the worse. A pretty girl must live or suffer—she has no choice!" Then returning to her former idea: "Much they deny themselves, your 'honest women.' They are worse, because nothing compels them. They have money to live on and amuse themselves, and they choose vicious lives of their own accord. They are the bad ones in reality."

She was standing near the bed of the distracted Yvette, who wanted to cry out "Help," to escape. Yvette wept aloud, like children who are whipped. The Marquise was silent and looked at her daughter, and, seeing her overwhelmed with despair, felt, herself, the pangs of grief, remorse, tenderness, and pity, and throwing herself upon the bed with open arms, she also began to sob and stammered:

"My poor little girl, my poor little girl, if you knew, how you were hurting me." And they wept together, a long while.

Then the Marquise, in whom grief could not long endure, softly rose, and gently said:

"Come, darling, it is unavoidable; what would you have? Nothing can be changed now. We must take life as it comes to us."

Yvette continued to weep. The blow had been too harsh and too unexpected to permit her to reflect and to recover at once.

Her mother resumed: "Now, get up and come down to breakfast, so that no one will notice anything."

The young girl shook her head as if to say, "No," without being able to speak. Then she said, with a slow voice full of sobs:

"No, mamma, you know what I said, I won't alter my determination. I shall not leave my room till they have gone. I never want to see one of those people again, never, never. If they come back, you will see no more of me."

The Marquise had dried her eyes, and wearied with emotion, she murmured:

"Come, reflect, be reasonable."

Then, after a moment's silence:

"Yes, you had better rest this morning. I will come up to see you this afternoon." And having kissed her daughter on the forehead, she went to dress herself, already calmed.

Yvette, as soon as her mother had disappeared, rose, and ran to bolt the door, to be alone, all alone; then she began to think. The chambermaid knocked about eleven o'clock, and asked through the door: "Madame the Marquise wants to know if Mademoiselle wishes anything, and what she will take for her breakfast."

Yvette answered: "I am not hungry, I only ask not to be disturbed."

And she remained in bed, just as if she had been ill. Toward three o'clock, some one knocked again. She asked:

"Who is there?"

It was her mother's voice which replied: "It is I, darling, I have come to see how you are."

She hesitated what she should do. She opened the door, and then went back to bed. The Marquise approached, and, speaking in low tones, as people do to a convalescent, said:

"Well, are you better? Won't you eat an egg?"

"No, thanks, nothing at all."

Madame Obardi sat down near the bed. They remained without saying anything, then, finally, as her daughter stayed quiet, with her hands inert upon the bedclothes, she asked:

"Don't you intend to get up?"

Yvette answered: "Yes, pretty soon."

Then in a grave and slow tone she said: "I have thought a great deal, mamma, and this—this is my resolution. The past is the past, let us speak no more of it. But the future shall be different or I know what is left for me to do. Now, let us say no more about it."

The Marquise, who thought the explanation finished, felt her impatience gaining a little. It was too much. This big goose of a girl ought to have known about things long ago. But she did not say anything in reply, only repeating:

"You are going to get up?"

"Yes, I am ready."

Then her mother became maid for her, bringing her stockings, her corset, and her skirts. Then she kissed her.

"Will you take a walk before dinner?"

"Yes, mamma."

And they took a stroll along the water, speaking only of commonplace things.

CHAPTER IV
FROM EMOTION TO PHILOSOPHY

The following day, early in the morning, Yvette went out alone to the place where Servigny had read her the history of the ants. She said to herself:

"I am not going away from this spot without having formed a resolution."

Before her, at her feet, the water flowed rapidly, filled with large bubbles which passed in silent flight with deep whirlings. She already had summed up the points of the situation and the means of extricating herself from it. What should she do if her mother would not accept the conditions which she had imposed, would not renounce her present way of living, her set of visitors—everything and go and hide with her in a distant land?

She might go alone, take flight, but where, and how? What would she live on? By working? At what? To whom should she apply to find work? And, then, the dull and humble life of working-women, daughters of the people, seemed a little disgraceful, unworthy of her. She thought of becoming a governess, like young girls in novels, and of becoming loved by the son of the house, and then marrying him. But to accomplish that she must have been of good birth, so that, when the exasperated father should approach her with having stolen his son's love, she might say in a proud voice:

"My name is Yvette Obardi."

She could not do this. And then, even that would have been a trite and threadbare method.

The convent was not worth much more. Besides, she felt no vocation for a religious life, having only an intermittent and fleeting piety. No one would save her by marrying her, being what she was! No aid was acceptable from a man, no possible issue, no definite resource.

And then she wished to do something energetic and really great and strong, which should serve as an example: so she resolved upon death.

She decided upon this step suddenly, but tranquilly, as if it were a journey, without reflecting, without looking at death, without understanding that it is the end without recommencement, the departure without return, the eternal farewell to earth and to this life.

She immediately settled on this extreme measure, with the lightness of young and excited souls, and she thought of the means which she would employ. But they all seemed to her painful and hazardous, and, furthermore, required a violence of action which repelled her.

She quickly abandoned the poniard and revolver, which might wound only, blind her or disfigure her, and which demanded a practiced and steady hand. She decided against the rope; it was so common, the poor man's way of suicide, ridiculous and ugly; and against water because she knew how to swim So poison remained—but which kind? Almost all of them cause suffering and incite vomitings. She did not want either of these things.

Then she thought of chloroform, having read in a newspaper how a young woman had managed to asphyxiate herself by this process. And she felt at once a sort of joy in her resolution, an inner pride, a sensation of bravery. People should see what she was, and what she was worth.

She returned to Bougival and went to a druggist, from whom she asked a little chloroform for a tooth which was aching. The man, who knew her, gave her a tiny bottle of the narcotic.

Then she set out on foot for Croissy, where she procured a second phial of poison. She obtained a third at Chaton, a fourth at Ruril, and got home late for breakfast.

As she was very hungry after this long walk, she ate heartily with the pleasurable appetite of people who have taken exercise.

Her mother, happy to see her so hungry, and now feeling tranquil herself, said to her as they left the table:

"All our friends are coming to spend Sunday with us. I have invited the Prince, the Chevalier, and Monsieur de Belvigne."

Yvette turned a little pale, but did not reply. She went out almost immediately, reached the railway station, and took a ticket for Paris. And during all the afternoon, she went from druggist to druggist, buying from each one a few drops of chloroform. She came back in the evening with her pockets full of little bottles.

She began the same system on the following day, and by chance found a chemist who gave her, at one stroke, a quarter of a liter. She did not go out on Saturday; it was a lowering and sultry day; she passed it entirely on the terrace, stretched on a long wicker-chair.

She thought of almost nothing, very resolute and very calm. She put on the next morning, a blue costume which was very becoming to her, wishing to look well. Then looking at herself in the glass, she suddenly said:

"To-morrow, I shall be dead." And a peculiar shudder passed over her body. "Dead! I shall speak no more, think no more, no one will see me more, and I shall never see anything again."

And she gazed attentively at her countenance, as if she had never observed it, examining especially her eyes, discovering a thousand things in herself, a secret character in her physiognomy which she had not known before, astonished to see herself, as if she had opposite her a strange person, a new friend.

She said to herself: "It is I, in the mirror, there. How queer it is to look at oneself. But without the mirror we would never know ourselves. Everybody else would know how we look, and we ourselves would know nothing."

She placed the heavy braids of her thick hair over her breast, following with her glance all her gestures, all her poses, and all her movements. "How pretty I am!" she thought. "Tomorrow I shall be dead, there, upon my bed." She looked at her bed, and seemed to see herself stretched out, white as the sheets.

Dead! In a week she would be nothing but dust, to dust returned! A horrible anguish oppressed her heart. The bright sunlight fell in floods upon the fields, and the soft morning air came in at the window.

She sat down thinking of it. Death! It was as if the world was going to disappear from her; but no, since nothing would be changed in the world, not even her bedroom. Yes, her room would remain just the same, with the same bed, the same chairs, the same toilette articles, but she would be forever gone, and no one would be sorry, except her mother, perhaps.

People would say: "How pretty she was! that little Yvette," and nothing more. And as she looked at her arm leaning on the arm of her chair, she thought again, ashes to ashes, dust to dust. And again a great shudder of horror ran over her whole body, and she did not know how she could disappear without the whole earth being blotted out, so much it seemed to her that she was a part of everything, of the fields, of the air, of the sunshine, of life itself.

There were bursts of laughter in the garden, a great noise of voices and of calls, the bustling gaiety of country house parties, and she recognized the sonorous tones of M. de Belvigne, singing:

"I am underneath thy window, Oh, deign to show thy face." She rose, without reflecting, and looked out. They all applauded. They were all five there, with two gentlemen whom she did not know.

She brusquely withdrew, annoyed by the thought that these men had come to amuse themselves at her mother's house, as at a public place.

The bell sounded for breakfast. "I will show them how to die," she said.

She went downstairs with a firm step, with something of the resolution of the Christian martyrs going into the circus, where the lions awaited them.

She pressed their hands, smiling in an affable but rather haughty manner. Servigny asked her:

"Are you less cross to-day, Mam'zelle?"

She answered in a severe and peculiar tone: "Today, I am going to commit follies. I am in my Paris mood, look out!"

Then turning toward Monsieur de Belvigne, she said:

"You shall be my escort, my little Malmsey. I will take you all after breakfast to the fete at Marly."

There was, in fact, a fete at Marly. They introduced the two newcomers to her, the Comte de Tamine and the Marquis de Briquetot.

During the meal, she said nothing further, strengthening herself to be gay in the afternoon, so that no one should guess anything,—so that they should be all the more astonished, and should say: "Who would have thought it? She seemed so happy, so contented! What does take place in those heads?"

She forced herself not to think of the evening, the chosen hour, when they should all be upon the terrace. She drank as much wine as she could stand, to nerve herself, and two little glasses of brandy, and she was flushed as she left the table, a little bewildered, heated in body and mind. It seemed to her that she was strengthened now, and resolved for everything.

"Let us start!" she cried. She took Monsieur de Belvigne's arm and set the pace for the others. "Come, you shall form my battalion, Servigny. I choose you as sergeant; you will keep outside the ranks, on the right. You will make the foreign guard march in front—the two exotics, the Prince, and the Chevalier—and in the rear the two recruits who have enlisted to-day. Come!"

They started. And Servigny began to imitate the trumpet, while the two newcomers made believe to beat the drum. Monsieur de Belvigne, a little confused, said in a low tone:

"Mademoiselle Yvette, be reasonable, you will compromise yourself."

She answered: "It is you whom I am compromising, Raisine. As for me, I don't care much about it. To-morrow it will not occur. So much the worse for you: you ought not to go out with girls like me."

They went through Bougival to the amazement of the passers-by. All turned to look at them; the citizens came to their doors; the travelers on the little railway which runs from Ruril to Marly jeered at them. The men on the platforms cried:

"To the water with them!"

Yvette marched with a military step, holding Belvigne by the arm, as a prisoner is led. She did not laugh; upon her features sat a pale seriousness, a sort of sinister calm. Servigny interrupted his trumpet blasts only to shout orders. The Prince and the Chevalier were greatly amused, finding all this very funny and in good taste. The two recruits drummed away continually.

When they arrived at the fete, they made a sensation. Girls applauded; young men jeered, and a stout gentleman with his wife on his arm said enviously: "There are some people who are full of fun."

Yvette saw the wooden horses and compelled Belvigne to mount at her right, while her squad scrambled upon the whirling beasts behind. When the time was up she refused to dismount, constraining her escort to take several more rides on the back of these children's animals, to the great delight of the public, who shouted jokes at them. Monsieur de Belvigne was livid and dizzy when he got off.

Then she began to wander among the booths. She forced all her men to get weighed among a crowd of spectators. She made them buy ridiculous toys which they had to carry in their hands. The Prince and the Chevalier began to think the joke was being carried too far. Servigny and the drummers, alone, did not seem to be discouraged.

They finally came to the end of the place. Then she gazed at her followers in a peculiar manner, with a shy and mischievous glance, and a strange fancy came to her mind. She drew them up on the bank of the river.

"Let the one who loves me the most jump into the water," she said.

Nobody leaped. A mob gathered behind them. Women in white aprons looked on in stupor. Two troopers, in red breeches, laughed loudly.

She repeated: "Then there is not one of you capable of jumping into the water at my desire?"

Servigny murmured: "Oh, yes, there is," and leaped feet foremost into the river. His plunge cast a splash over as far as Yvette's feet. A murmur of astonishment and gaiety arose in the crowd.

Then the young girl picked up from the ground a little piece of wood, and throwing it into the stream: "Fetch it," she cried.

The young man began to swim, and seizing the floating stick in his mouth, like a dog, he brought it ashore, and then climbing the bank he kneeled on one knee to present it.

Yvette took it. "You are handsome," said she, and with a friendly stroke, she caressed his hair.

A stout woman indignantly exclaimed: "Are such things possible!"

Another woman said: "Can people amuse themselves like that!"

A man remarked: "I would not take a plunge for that sort of a girl."

She again took Belvigne's arm, exclaiming in his face: "You are a goose, my friend; you don't know what you missed."

They now returned. She cast vexed looks on the passers-by. "How stupid all these people seem," she said. Then raising her eyes to the countenance of her companion, she added: "You, too, like all the rest."

M. de Belvigne bowed. Turning around she saw that the Prince and the Chevalier had disappeared. Servigny, dejected and dripping, ceased playing on the trumpet, and walked with a gloomy air at the side of the two wearied young men, who also had stopped the drum playing. She began to laugh dryly, saying:

"You seem to have had enough; nevertheless, that is what you call having a good time, isn't it? You came for that; I have given you your money's worth."

Then she walked on, saying nothing further; and suddenly Belvigne perceived that she was weeping. Astounded, he inquired:

"What is the matter?"

She murmured: "Let me alone, it does not concern you."

But he insisted, like a fool: "Oh, Mademoiselle, come, what is the matter, has anyone annoyed you?"

She repeated impatiently: "Will you keep still?"

Then suddenly, no longer able to resist the despairing sorrow which drowned her heart, she began to sob so violently, that she could no longer walk. She covered her face with her hands, panting for breath, choked by the violence of her despair.

Belvigne stood still at her side, quite bewildered, repeating: "I don't understand this at all."

But Servigny brusquely came forward: "Let us go home, Mam'zelle, so that people may not see you weeping in the street. Why do you perpetrate follies like that when they only make you sad?"

And taking her arm he drew her forward. But as soon as they reached the iron gate of the villa she began to run, crossed the garden, and went upstairs, and shut herself in her room. She did not appear again until the dinner hour, very pale and serious. Servigny had bought from a country storekeeper a workingman's costume, with velvet pantaloons, a flowered waistcoat and a blouse, and he adopted the local dialect. Yvette was in a hurry for them to finish, feeling her courage ebbing. As soon as the coffee was served she went to her room again.

She heard the merry voices beneath her window. The Chevalier was making equivocal jokes, foreign witticisms, vulgar and clumsy. She listened, in despair. Servigny, just a bit tipsy, was imitating the common workingman, calling the Marquise "the Missus." And all of a sudden he said to Saval: "Well, Boss?" That caused a general laugh.

Then Yvette decided. She first took a sheet of paper and wrote:

"Bougival, Sunday, nine o'clock in the evening.
"I die so that I may not become a kept woman.

"YVETTE."

Then in a postscript:

"Adieu, my dear mother, pardon."

She sealed the envelope, and addressed it to the Marquise Obardi.

Then she rolled her long chair near the window, drew a little table within reach of her hand, and placed upon it the big bottle of chloroform beside a handful of wadding.

A great rose-tree covered with flowers, climbing as high as her window, exhaled in the night a soft and gentle perfume, in light breaths; and she stood for a moment enjoying it. The moon, in its first quarter, was floating in the dark sky, a little ragged at the left, and veiled at times by slight mists.

Yvette thought: "I am going to die!" And her heart, swollen with sobs, nearly bursting, almost suffocated her. She felt in her a need of asking mercy from some one, of being saved, of being loved.

The voice of Servigny aroused her. He was telling an improper story, which was constantly interrupted by bursts of laughter. The Marquise herself laughed louder than the others.

"There is nobody like him for telling that sort of thing," she said, laughing.

Yvette took the bottle, uncorked it, and poured a little of the liquid on the cotton. A strong, sweet, strange odor arose; and as she brought the piece of cotton to her lips, the fumes entered her throat and made her cough.

Then shutting her mouth, she began to inhale it. She took in long breaths of this deadly vapor, closing her eyes, and forcing herself to stifle in her mind all thoughts, so that she might not reflect, that she might know nothing more.

It seemed to her at first that her chest was growing larger, was expanding, and that her soul, recently heavy and burdened with grief, was becoming light, light, as if the weight which overwhelmed her was lifted, wafted away. Something lively and agreeable penetrated even to the extremities of her limbs, even to the tips of her toes and fingers and entered her flesh, a sort of dreamy intoxication, of soft fever. She saw that the cotton was dry, and she was astonished that she was not already dead. Her senses seemed more acute, more subtle, more alert. She heard the lowest whisper on the terrace. Prince Kravalow was telling how he had killed an Austrian general in a duel.

Then, further off, in the fields, she heard the noise of the night, the occasional barkings of a dog, the short cry of the frogs, the almost imperceptible rustling of the leaves.

She took the bottle again, and saturated once more the little piece of wadding; then she began to breathe in the fumes again. For a few moments she felt nothing; then that soft and soothing feeling of comfort which she had experienced before enveloped her.

Twice she poured more chloroform upon the cotton, eager now for that physical and mental sensation, that dreamy torpor, which bewildered her soul.

It seemed to her that she had no more bones, flesh, legs, or arms. The drug had gently taken all these away from her, without her perceiving it. The chloroform had drawn away her body, leaving her only her mind, more awakened, more active, larger, and more free than she had ever felt it.

She recalled a thousand forgotten things, little details of her childhood, trifles which had given her pleasure. Endowed suddenly with an awakened agility, her mind leaped to the most diverse ideas, ran through a thousand adventures, wandered in the past, and lost itself in the hoped-for events of the future. And her lively and careless thoughts had a sensuous charm: she experienced a divine pleasure in dreaming thus.

She still heard the voices, but she could no longer distinguish the words, which to her seemed to have a different meaning. She was in a kind of strange and changing fairyland.

She was on a great boat which floated through a beautiful country, all covered with flowers. She saw people on the shore, and these people spoke very loudly; then she was again on land, without asking how, and Servigny, clad as a prince, came to seek her, to take her to a bull-fight.

The streets were filled with passers-by, who were talking, and she heard conversations which did not astonish her, as if she had known the people, for through her dreamy intoxication, she still heard her mother's friends laughing and talking on the terrace.

Then everything became vague. Then she awakened, deliciously benumbed, and she could hardly remember what had happened.

So, she was not yet dead. But she felt so calm, in such a state of physical comfort, that she was not in haste to finish with it—she wanted to make this exquisite drowsiness last forever.

She breathed slowly and looked at the moon, opposite her, above the trees. Something had changed in her spirit. She no longer thought as she had done just now. The chloroform quieting her body and her soul had calmed her grief and lulled her desire to die.

Why should she not live? Why should she not be loved? Why should she not lead a happy life? Everything appeared possible to her now, and easy and certain. Everything in life was sweet, everything was charming. But as she wished to dream on still, she poured more of the dream-water on the cotton and began to breathe it in again, stopping at times, so as not to absorb too much of it and die.

She looked at the moon and saw in it a face, a woman's face. She began to scorn the country in the fanciful intoxication of the drug. That face swung in the sky; then it sang, it sang with a well-known voice the alleluia of love.

It was the Marquise, who had come in and seated herself at the piano.

Yvette had wings now. She was flying through a clear night, above the wood and streams. She was flying with delight, opening and closing her wings, borne by the wind as by a caress. She moved in the air, which kissed her skin, and she went so fast, so fast, that she had no time to see anything beneath her, and she found herself seated on the bank of a pond with a line in her hand; she was fishing.

Something pulled on the cord, and when she drew it out of the water, it bore a magnificent pearl necklace, which she had longed for some time ago. She was not at all astonished at this deed, and she looked at Servigny, who had come to her side—she knew not how. He was fishing also, and drew out of the river a wooden horse.

Then she had anew the feeling of awaking, and she heard some one calling down stairs. Her mother had said:

"Put out the candle." Then Servigny's voice rose, clear and jesting:

"Put out your candle, Mam'zelle Yvette."

And all took up the chorus: "Mam'zelle Yvette, put out your candle."

She again poured chloroform on the cotton, but, as she did not want to die, she placed it far enough from her face to breathe the fresh air, while nevertheless her room was filled with the asphyxiating odor of the narcotic, for she knew that some one was coming, and taking a suitable posture, a pose of the dead, she waited.

The Marquise said: "I am a little uneasy! That foolish child has gone to sleep leaving the light on her table. I will send Clemence to put it out, and to shut the balcony window, which is wide open."

And soon the maid rapped on the door calling: "Mademoiselle, Mademoiselle!" After a moment's silence, she repeated: "Mademoiselle, Madame the Marquise begs you to put out your candle and shut the window."

Clemence waited a little, then knocked louder, and cried:

"Mademoiselle, Mademoiselle!"

As Yvette did not reply, the servant went away and reported to the Marquise:

"Mademoiselle must have gone to sleep, her door is bolted, and I could not awaken her."

Madame Obardi murmured:

"But she must not stay like that,"

Then, at the suggestion of Servigny, they all gathered under the window, shouting in chorus:

"Hip! hip! hurrah! Mam'zelle Yvette."

Their clamor rose in the calm night, through the transparent air beneath the moon, over the sleeping country; and they heard it die away in the distance like the sound of a disappearing train.

As Yvette did not answer the Marquise said: "I only hope that nothing has happened. I am beginning to be afraid."

Then Servigny, plucking red roses from a big rosebush trained along the wall and buds not yet opened, began to throw them into the room through the window.

At the first rose that fell at her side, Yvette started and almost cried out. Others fell upon her dress, others upon her hair, while others going over her head fell upon the bed, covering it with a rain of flowers.

The Marquise, in a choking voice, cried: "Come, Yvette, answer."

Then Servigny declared: "Truly this is not natural; I am going to climb up by the balcony."

But the Chevalier grew indignant.

"Now, let me do it," he said. "It is a great favor I ask; it is too good a means, and too good a time to obtain a rendezvous."

All the rest, who thought the young girl was joking, cried: "We protest! He shall not climb up."

But the Marquise, disturbed, repeated: "And yet some one must go and see."

The Prince exclaimed with a dramatic gesture:

"She favors the Duke, we are betrayed."

"Let us toss a coin to see who shall go up," said the Chevalier. He took a five-franc piece from his pocket, and began with the Prince.

"Tail," said he. It was head.

The Prince tossed the coin in his turn saying to Saval: "Call, Monsieur."

Saval called "Head." It was tail.

The Prince then gave all the others a chance, and they all lost.

Servigny, who was standing opposite him, exclaimed in his insolent way: "PARBLEU! he is cheating!"

The Russian put his hand on his heart and held out the gold piece to his rival, saying: "Toss it yourself, my dear Duke."

Servigny took it and spinning it up, said: "Head." It was tail.

He bowed and pointing to the pillar of the balcony said: "Climb up, Prince." But the Prince looked about him with a disturbed air.

"What are you looking for?" asked the Chevalier.

"Well,—I—would—like—a ladder." A general laugh followed.

Saval, advancing, said: "We will help you."

He lifted him in his arms, as strong as those of Hercules, telling him:

"Now climb to that balcony."

The Prince immediately clung to it, and, Saval letting him go, he swung there, suspended in the air, moving his legs in empty space.

Then Servigny, seeing his struggling legs which sought a resting place, pulled them downward with all his strength; the hands lost their grip and the Prince fell in a heap on Monsieur de Belvigne, who was coming to aid him. "Whose turn next?" asked Servigny. No one claimed the privilege.

"Come, Belvigne, courage!"

"Thank you, my dear boy, I am thinking of my bones."

"Come, Chevalier, you must be used to scaling walls."

"I give my place to you, my dear Duke."

"Ha, ha, that is just what I expected."

Servigny, with a keen eye, turned to the pillar. Then with a leap, clinging to the balcony, he drew himself up like a gymnast and climbed over the balustrade.

All the spectators, gazing at him, applauded. But he immediately reappeared, calling:

"Come, quick! Come, quick! Yvette is unconscious." The Marquise uttered a loud cry, and rushed for the stairs.

The young girl, her eyes closed, pretended to be dead. Her mother entered distracted, and threw her self upon her.

"Tell me what is the matter with her, what is the matter with her?"

Servigny picked up the bottle of chloroform which had fallen upon the floor.

"She has drugged herself," said he.

He placed his ear to her heart; then he added:

"But she is not dead; we can resuscitate her. Have you any ammonia?"

The maid, bewildered, repeated: "Any what, Monsieur?"

"Any smelling-salts."

"Yes, Monsieur." "Bring them at once, and leave the door open to make a draft of air."

The Marquise, on her knees, was sobbing: "Yvette! Yvette, my daughter, my daughter, listen, answer me, Yvette, my child. Oh, my God! my God! what has she done?"

The men, frightened, moved about without speaking, bringing water, towels, glasses, and vinegar. Some one said: "She ought to be undressed." And the Marquise, who had lost her head, tried to undress her daughter; but did not know what she was doing. Her hands trembled and faltered, and she groaned:

"I cannot,—I cannot—"

The maid had come back bringing a druggist's bottle which Servigny opened and from which he poured out half upon a handkerchief. Then he applied it to Yvette's nose, causing her to choke.

"Good, she breathes," said he. "It will be nothing."

And he bathed her temples, cheeks, and neck with the pungent liquid.

Then he made a sign to the maid to unlace the girl, and when she had nothing more on than a skirt over her chemise, he raised her in his arms and carried her to the bed, quivering, moved by the odor and contact of her flesh. Then she was placed in bed. He arose very pale.

"She will come to herself," he said, "it is nothing." For he had heard her breathe in a continuous and regular way. But seeing all the men with their eyes fixed on Yvette in bed, he was seized with a jealous irritation, and advanced toward them. "Gentlemen," he said, "there are too many of us in this room; be kind enough to leave us alone,—Monsieur Saval and me—with the Marquise."

He spoke in a tone which was dry and full of authority.

Madame Obardi had grasped her lover, and with her head uplifted toward him she cried to him:

"Save her, oh, save her!"

But Servigny turning around saw a letter on the table. He seized it with a rapid movement, and read the address. He understood and thought: "Perhaps it would be better if the Marquise should not know of this," and tearing open the envelope, he devoured at a glance the two lines it contained:

"I die so that I may not become a kept woman."
"Yvette."

"Adieu, my dear mother, pardon."

"The devil!" he thought, "this calls for reflection." And he hid the letter in his pocket.

Then he approached the bed, and immediately the thought came to him that the young girl had regained consciousness but that she dared not show it, from shame, from humiliation, and from fear of questioning. The Marquise had fallen on her knees now, and was weeping, her head on the foot of the bed. Suddenly she exclaimed:

"A doctor, we must have a doctor!"

But Servigny, who had just said something in a low tone to Saval, replied to her: "No, it is all over. Come, go out a minute, just a minute, and I promise you that she will kiss you when you come back." And the Baron, taking Madame Obardi by the arm, led her from the room.

Then Servigny, sitting-by the bed, took Yvette's hand and said: "Mam'zelle, listen to me."

She did not answer. She felt so well, so soft and warm in bed, that she would have liked never to move, never to speak, and to live like that forever. An infinite comfort had encompassed her, a comfort the like of which she had never experienced.

The mild night air coming in by velvety breaths touched her temples in an exquisite almost imperceptible way. It was a caress like a kiss of the wind, like the soft and refreshing breath of a fan made of all the leaves of the trees and of all the shadows of the night, of the mist of rivers, and of all the flowers too, for the roses tossed up from below into her room and upon her bed, and the roses climbing at her balcony, mingled their heavy perfume with the healthful savor of the evening breeze.

She drank in this air which was so good, her eyes closed, her heart reposing in the yet pervading intoxication of the drug, and she had no longer at all the desire to die, but a strong, imperious wish to live, to be happy—no matter how—to be loved, yes, to be loved.

Servigny repeated: "Mam'zelle Yvette, listen to me."

And she decided to open her eyes.

He continued, as he saw her reviving: "Come! Come! what does this nonsense mean?"

She murmured: "My poor Muscade, I was so unhappy."

He squeezed her hand: "And that led you into a pretty scrape! Come, you must promise me not to try it again."

She did not reply, but nodded her head slightly with an almost imperceptible smile. He drew from his pocket the letter which he had found on the table:

"Had I better show this to your mother?"

She shook her head, no. He knew not what more to say for the situation seemed to him without an outlet. So he murmured:

"My dear child, everyone has hard things to bear. I understand your sorrow and I promise you—"

She stammered: "You are good."

They were silent. He looked at her. She had in her glance something of tenderness, of weakness; and suddenly she raised both her arms, as if she would draw him to her; he bent over her, feeling that she called him, and their lips met.

For a long time they remained thus, their eyes closed.

But, knowing that he would lose his head, he drew away. She smiled at him now, most tenderly; and, with both her hands clinging to his shoulders, she held him.

"I am going to call your mother," he said.

She murmured: "Just a second more. I am so happy."

Then after a silence, she said in a tone so low that it could scarcely be heard: "Will you love me very much? Tell me!"

He kneeled beside her bed, and kissing the hand she had given him, said: "I adore you." But some one was walking near the door. He arose with a bound, and called in his ordinary voice, which seemed nevertheless a little ironical: "You may come in. It is all right now."

The Marquise threw herself on her daughter, with both arms open, and clasped her frantically, covering her countenance with tears, while Servigny with radiant soul and quivering body went out upon the balcony to breathe the fresh air of the night, humming to himself the old couplet:

> "A woman changeth oft her mind:
> Yet fools still trust in womankind."